***"I don't want to let you go,"* Ken said.**

Millie felt her pulse quicken at his words.

"If we're together for two seconds, I want to touch you," he murmured. Blood thundered in his veins as he bent his head and covered her mouth with his own. She was soft, sweet, hot to his touch. There was a promise given in each kiss that made him demand more and more.

Millie burned with longing that had been bottled up for too many years, too many lonely nights. Ken pulled her to him, tightening his arms around her waist. She gasped, clinging to him, trembling in the embrace of a man she barely knew. He was on fire with need for her, and she was powerless to stop him . . .

WHAT ARE *LOVESWEPT* ROMANCES?

They are stories of true romance and touching emotion. We believe those two very important ingredients are constants in our highly sensual and very believable stories in the *LOVESWEPT* line. Our goal is to give you, the reader, stories of consistently high quality that may sometimes make you laugh, sometimes make you cry, but are always fresh and creative and contain many delightful surprises within their pages.

Most romance fans read an enormous number of books. Those they truly love, they keep. Others may be traded with friends and soon forgotten. We hope that each *LOVESWEPT* romance will be a treasure—a "keeper." We will always try to publish

LOVE STORIES YOU'LL NEVER FORGET
BY AUTHORS YOU'LL ALWAYS REMEMBER

The Editors

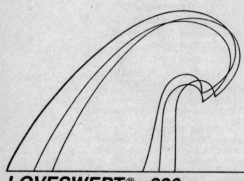

LOVESWEPT® • 226

Sara Orwig
Out of the Mist

BANTAM BOOKS
TORONTO • NEW YORK • LONDON • SYDNEY • AUCKLAND

OUT OF THE MIST
A Bantam Book / December 1987

If you would be interested in receiving protective vinyl
covers for your Loveswept books, please write to this address
for information:

Loveswept
Bantam Books
P.O. Box 985
Hicksville, NY 11802

ISBN 0-553-21857-3

Published simultaneously in the United States and Canada

Bantam Books are published by Bantam Books, Inc. Its trademark, consisting of the words "Bantam Books" and the por-
trayal of a rooster, is Registered in U.S. Patent and Trademark
Office and in other countries. Marca Registrada. Bantam
Books, Inc., 666 Fifth Avenue, New York, New York 10103.

PRINTED IN THE UNITED STATES OF AMERICA

O   0 9 8 7 6 5 4 3 2 1

One

The wide lobby of the country club was filled with people leaving a reception and cocktail party that had been given by civic leaders for the promotion of the metropolitan Colorado city. Potted palms graced several corners of the lobby, and the elegant furniture was comfortable, but most chairs were empty because the crowd had shifted toward the front doors. A member of City Beautiful as well as Friends of the Library, Millie Blake had attended the function and heard ideas on improving and promoting the city during the coming year. Now the group was breaking up, and she was going home to a quiet dinner.

After smoothing a stray tendril of brown hair into the bun fastened at the back of her head, she shrugged into her heavy, navy wool coat. Glancing outside at the chilly December night and the winter landscape, Millie noticed how the snow sparkled beneath lamps in the parking lot. The

Christmas lights that decorated the country club grounds added a note of cheer in spite of a misty fog that made visibility poor.

"Sure you don't want to go to a movie?" Millie's friend Claire Rainy asked.

"Thanks, but I'll pass tonight. The weather's too bad." As she stood in the doorway pulling on her gloves, she saw a tall man striding across the parking lot, mist shrouding his figure. He slipped on a patch of ice, righted himself with ease, and went striding on, unaware that something had fallen from the pocket of his topcoat.

A green bill fluttered against the tire of a parked car, and she realized the man had dropped his billfold.

"Bye, Millie. Call me soon and we'll make plans to go to dinner."

"Okay. Good night, Claire," she called over her shoulder. Pushing swiftly through the door, Millie rushed to get the billfold.

"Mister! Hey, Mister!" she called, her breath vaporizing in the icy air. Scooping up the billfold, she paused momentarily, her attention caught. The wallet was stuffed with money, more than she had ever held at one time, she suspected. Then she noticed a fifty-dollar bill lying in the snow. She scooped it up and jammed it back into the billfold.

"Mister!" she yelled, while the man bent over to unlock the door of a car. He glanced over his shoulder at her, and she waved, then she hurried to get another fifty that had lodged against a tire.

She hurried over to the man, and as she approached she held out the billfold and the fifty she had just picked up.

"You dropped this."

A startled look crossed his features, and his hand flew to his overcoat pocket. "Damn. The pockets on this coat—thanks! I stopped in the lobby to get chewing gum and jammed my wallet into my coat pocket. I should have known better. These pockets aren't very deep, and with gloves on, I probably didn't get it all the way in."

He looked at her with curiosity in his clear blue eyes. "I'm Ken Holloway."

"Yes, I know," she said, and waved her hand at the country club, realizing he wouldn't remember meeting her in the large group of new people to whom he'd been introduced this evening. Most people knew him because he was in town on a business deal that involved one of the large local industries. "I'm Millie Blake," she added, thinking Mr. Ken Holloway was the most handsome man she had ever seen, with his dark, almost indigo-blue eyes and thick, wavy black hair.

He shook her hand in a firm grip then pulled out some bills, holding them out to her.

"Listen, thanks," he said, offering her the cash.

"Oh, no! That's not necessary." She smiled at him while self-consciously her hand drifted to her cheek, lightly touching a long scar. "I don't want anything. I simply saw you drop your billfold and returned it to you."

"Come on. You could have walked off with it. And many people would have. Let me say thanks."

"You did say thanks," she said. "That's sufficient."

"Okay," he said, thrusting the bills back into the billfold. He tugged off a glove to unbutton his coat and slipped the wallet into his hip pocket. She stood watching him, thinking he was nice to look at. "What's your address, Millie Blake?" he asked.

"I live in Strawberry Mountain," she said, naming the suburban area beyond the northern limits of the city that included more than one mountain.

"Ah!" he said with satisfaction, as if he recognized the area she had mentioned. "Whereabouts in Strawberry Mountain?" he asked with amusement, flashing her a smile that warmed the cold night.

"Ten Snowy Lane," she said, knowing she wouldn't hesitate to tell him her phone number, her age, her vital statistics, or anything else he inquired about. She suspected he was asking because he intended to send her some token of his thanks. "Well, good night," she said, suddenly feeling awkward.

"Good night and thanks again," he said, then climbed into his car as she turned to walk away. She sighed and shoved her hands into her pockets after adjusting the purse she had slung over her shoulder.

A car backed out and swung around beside her, and Claire lowered the window. "Come on—it won't hurt you to go with me to Tonio's for pizza."

"Okay! Okay!" Millie said, laughing and throwing up her hands. "But I don't want to be out late; the weather's bad."

"Sure. Leave your car here. I'll bring you back."

Millie climbed into Claire's car, seeing Ken Holloway's black Lincoln turn out of the parking lot.

Later that night as she was driving home, fog drifted ahead in the road like tumbling, fallen clouds, obscuring visibility beyond a few yards. The car's headlights glinted on the tall pines and spruce lining the road; an opaque grayness obliterated all else. Gripping the steering wheel of her six-year-old red Renault as she drove, Millie wasn't unduly alarmed, because she knew every twist and turn of the Colorado highway up the mountainside to her house. The first twinge of concern surfaced when she heard the high wail of a siren. When she came to a curve in the road, she glanced to her right. She should have been able to see down the mountainside, but couldn't now because of the fog.

Houses were scattered from the base to the top of the mountain. Some were elegant homes nestled back in the pines, others were simple houses like Millie's, and there were a few one-room log cabins used by summer fishermen.

After the next bend in the road she caught sight of an orange glow. Black smoke pierced the fog, a seemingly impossible occurrence in such damp weather. Someone's home was on fire, and she felt a momentary rush of sympathy for the owner and a glimmer of hope that the fire department could control it quickly. It was too damp to worry about the blaze spreading, so she continued on, her concentration returning to the road ahead as she searched for the turn to her house. Her gaze swept the snow-covered, foggy slopes, shifting for a second to the rearview mirror, where she caught a glimpse of her own wide-eyed reflection, her hazel eyes, and straight, thin nose.

Gravel crunched under the tires as she swung the car into her driveway. She was sure of her surroundings now and no longer had to worry.

Within seconds the garage and house loomed ahead, appearing out of the mists. When she cut the motor and stepped outside, sirens were still wailing, eerie in the silence. She missed the usual greeting of her dog, Drifter, who had been sick and was at the veterinarian's. Snow crunched underfoot with each step as she moved through the darkness toward the house.

In spite of the late hour and heavy mist Millie seldom had qualms about coming home alone. When she had bought the house two years earlier, she had quickly dismissed her fears over living in such isolation, but tonight as she fumbled for her key she felt a strange prickling of her skin. She decided it was because she didn't have Drifter with her to discourage prowlers.

Sirens continued to blare, some sounding closer now, and for a moment she paused, wondering what was happening at the burning house down the mountain. Shrugging away her own questions, she tried to turn the key and realized the door was already unlocked. She frowned, momentarily disconcerted over the unlocked door, because she nearly always remembered to lock it when she left for the day.

She switched on a light and closed the kitchen door behind her, slipping the lock in place and looking around the bright yellow kitchen. Nothing was disturbed, and she forgot about the unlocked door as she hung up her coat and stuffed her gloves into the pockets.

The mewling of the puppies in the box in the corner of the kitchen greeted her, and she walked over to look down at them. A scraping sound suddenly came from another part of the house, and Millie's head jerked up, her eyes narrowing and her ears straining to hear.

Everything was silent for about two seconds, then a puppy whined and another bit the paper in the bottom of the box, tearing a piece loose and shaking it.

She smiled, deciding she was jumping at every little noise because Drifter wasn't there.

"Some help you fellows are!" she teased the pups, staring at the three that remained of the six she had discovered abandoned on the road. She picked up one whining pup and held him, wondering what breed he was with his mottled black and brown hair.

"Brave doggie! You're supposed to stand watch, not cry to be held. Now, settle down. You've got food, a warm bed, and a warm house." She put the pup back into the box, turned off the kitchen light, and headed for her room. Another twinge of uneasiness hit her, but she was reassured when she walked into the familiar pink bedroom and took in the undisturbed four-poster bed and mahogany furniture. She switched on a bedside lamp and pulled off her coat, humming a Christmas carol to herself while she undressed.

Knowing her navy suit needed to go to the cleaners, she placed it on a chair and tossed her white blouse and underclothes into a clothes hamper. She pulled a pink flannel nightgown out of a drawer and slipped it over her head.

The sharp steady rise of a siren broke the silence, and Millie paused. The screaming noise became louder, closer. It sounded as if the police were on her road—the closest house was over half a mile up the mountain. Abruptly the sound stopped, and as she marched toward the bathroom to brush her teeth the doorbell rang.

She had been right—the sirens had been on her road. With a frown she walked to the closet to get her robe. Opening the door, she raised her hand to reach for the familiar blue quilted robe, and she froze in shock.

A man was staring at her from inside the closet. For an instant both of them were immobile with surprise. Then he moved.

Before the scream that rose to her throat could become a sound, he spun her around, clamping a hand over her mouth as he pulled her tightly up against him and held her in an iron grip.

Her heart seemed to stop beating, slamming against her ribs with such force, it took her breath away. In the seconds before he had acted, she had formed a brief, indelible memory of tousled black hair, a cut on his cheek, mud-spattered clothing, and a pistol—and she *knew* him! It was Ken Holloway.

"Please let me hide here," a deep voice said quietly in her ear. "I didn't mean to startle you. The police are probably at the door."

As if to emphasize his words the bell rang repeatedly, and they heard an insistent knock.

He removed his hand, and her shock subsided a fraction. He stepped out of the closet, facing her in the dim glow of light from the small dresser lamp.

"They think I murdered a man. I *didn't* shoot him and I don't want to turn myself in. I won't hurt you, but will you help me? Please?"

The question hung in the air while the knocking continued. Ken Holloway's appearance wasn't reassuring. She stared at the gun in his hand. He followed her gaze, hastily laying the weapon on a bedside table and holding up his empty hands. "Please."

Reacting out of emotion and not intelligence, she nodded.

He closed his eyes in relief.

"I need my robe," she tried to say, but the words came out as a hoarse, breathless whisper.

"Here," he snapped, and thrust the robe into her hands. She glimpsed at his wrist, which was smudged with mud on the once-white cuff of his shirt, and at a thin gold watchband.

"I better answer the door." She pulled on the robe as she hurried to the door. Opening it, she came face to face with two policemen.

"Strawberry Mountain Police, Miss Blake. Sorry to disturb you so late at night. I'm Sergeant Willis, and this is Officer Akins."

"That's all right. I heard the sirens," she said, feeling just as stunned by her agreement to help Ken Holloway as by the surprise of finding him in her closet.

"There's been a murder at the Poplin place, and we think the suspect is in the area. Have you seen a stranger?"

"No, I haven't." She could answer honestly because Ken Holloway wasn't a stranger; she knew his identity full well.

"Are you here alone?"

"Do you count three puppies?" she asked, and forced a smile.

"Lock yourself in and check through your house right away, while we're still close. We think he's armed and dangerous." Officer Akins held out a picture. "Have you seen this man?"

She stared at a snapshot of a handsome, smiling, black-haired man in a dark suit. He looked like an ad for a line of men's designer shirts or cologne, not as if he belonged on a wanted poster. And not like the man in her closet.

"Miss? You think you've seen him?"

"Oh!" She hadn't realized how long she had hesitated. "I haven't seen a man who looks like the one in the picture," she said, thinking Ken bore little resemblance now to his picture. "He doesn't look like a murderer."

They gave her a patient, forbearing look. "If you have any trouble or hear someone prowling around, call the station. We'll be in the neighborhood for hours. We're setting up roadblocks to cordon off the area, and I don't think he'll get far, so be very careful."

"I will."

"Do you mind if we search your yard?"

"No, of course not," she said quickly.

"If you need us, just holler," one of the officers said. As they left she stared at their broad backs and wondered if she was making the most colossal mistake of her life.

Murder. She could so easily call the policemen back and get help. She recalled Ken Holloway's whisper when he had held her tightly in the closet: *"Please let me hide here."*

He hadn't sounded vicious, just desperate. She closed the door and turned around.

He stood across the room from her, leaning against the wall, and for the first time she could see him clearly. It wasn't reassuring. His blue eyes had a cold look to them. He was bruised; his hand and jaw, cut. Leaves and mud were stuck to him. There was a harshness to his handsome features, and he bore little resemblance to the smiling man she had met earlier in the evening.

Her heart began to skip beats as she questioned whether she had done the right thing.

A light from outside where the police were searching the grounds swept across the darkened kitchen windows, and she followed his glance, seeing a circle of yellow sweep up and down on the window shade.

Ken Holloway glanced toward the kitchen and stiffened. They both stared at the back door as a policeman tried the knob.

"You should do what he said. Walk through the house and turn on lights as if you're checking for a prowler."

Quickly she went through her small one-bedroom house, turning on lights, aware of the man behind her. He barely made a sound, but his presence gave her a cold, prickly feeling across the back of her neck. In spite of the tall Christmas tree, its bright decorations, and a pile of packages on the floor beneath it, the living room, which was usually so cheerful, looked uninviting and empty.

Finally she had turned on lights in every room in the house.

"You're doing fine," he said. "I'll try to repay you someday. I'll be gone as soon as I can leave safely, but you heard them—roadblocks. I'm afraid you have me on your hands for a time."

For the first time she noticed a cut on his neck and his bloody hand. "You're hurt."

"It's nothing, just scratches. I got cut on a fence I climbed. This is the worst." He took off his suitcoat and turned, and she saw the dark streak of blood on his tattered shirt. His voice was deep and firm. "I'm innocent."

Her head came up, and when she looked into his eyes, she suddenly was caught by his gaze. Some indefinable quality about him seemed to compel her to face him as long as he willed her to.

"I'm Ken Holloway, in case you don't remember my name."

"I remember you, Mr. Holloway," she said dryly, her fear diminishing a fraction in the routine of social amenities. "And I'm Millie Blake, if you don't remember."

His whole demeanor changed. The coldness momentarily left his eyes, creases appeared in his cheeks, and his voice was friendly. "Of course, I remember."

He was changing like a chameleon tossed onto a patchwork quilt. Right before her eyes the dangerous, distraught man who had startled her so badly was becoming the friendly, charming man she had encountered earlier.

"Did you come here on purpose?" she asked suddenly. She realized that she had told him her address when they'd first met.

"Your house was in the vicinity. I'll have to

admit when I saw the number on your mailbox, I remembered it was your address. How could I forget someone who returned my money to me?" He laughed, and the transformation was complete. In spite of the dirt and cuts and bruises and his disheveled appearance, he was an incredibly appealing man.

"You should be more trusting, Mr. Holloway."

She was rewarded with a lopsided grin that would have melted icicles. "Thank heaven I found your house."

Her gaze drifted over him, and all she saw was another human in need.

"You need help. I'll show you to the bathroom, so you can clean and disinfect your cuts."

As if he hadn't heard what she'd said, he continued to stare at her. Something indefinable flickered in the depths of his eyes, and she became aware of herself as a woman. The feeling was novel and disturbing, and now she was uneasy in a new way.

"Please," she whispered without realizing what she had said, her hand drifting to the scar on her cheek. "If you'll follow me." She marched past him to her bedroom, waving her hand toward the open door of the bathroom.

He casually dropped his jacket on the bed, then slipped off his tie. There was a male aura about him that overwhelmed Millie. He began to unbutton his shirt, and she looked away quickly, then went into the hall and reached into the linen closet to get him a clean towel and washcloth. "Here. There's disinfectant, gauze, and bandages in the cabinet, if you need any."

"Sure, thanks," he said, his warm fingers brushing hers as he took the towel and cloth. She was conscious of each touch, of his presence, and then she realized he was blocking her way to the door.

"Thanks for what you're doing."

She nodded and wanted to slip past him, but he wouldn't move.

"I'm bothering you." His voice dropped a notch. "Don't be afraid of me."

She waved her hands helplessly. "Will you move out of my way, please?"

"Sure."

Relieved to escape his presence, she returned to her bedroom, hearing him swear behind her. She turned and saw him shake his hand, then plunge it under a stream of water.

"Can you help with my back?"

She didn't want to touch his back, but she nodded and went to him, taking the wet cloth from his hand. As she gently wiped away blood he talked.

"I was climbing over a chain-link fence," he said, "and the damn thing gave way, and I fell. That's how I got these cuts."

She tried not to hurt him, cleaning around the long cut that ran across the left side of his back and down below his belt. His skin was smooth and tanned, and she wondered where he'd spent the winter to get so much sun.

"I'm not a murderer," he said firmly. "I didn't commit a crime. I was framed. . . ."

"This cut is deep. You may need stitches."

"I'll be okay."

"Shouldn't you go to the police for help if you're innocent?"

His profile was to her as he tried to put a bandage over the cut on his hand, and she noticed the thickness and length of his eyelashes.

"No. I can't go to the police. If you'll help me, I promise to pay you, Miss Blake," Ken said, feeling as if he were with one of his schoolteachers. He couldn't remember another woman near his own age whom he felt compelled to address as Miss or Mrs., but Miss Blake came more easily than Millie. In spite of her kindness there was a formidable aloofness to her that put an invisible barrier around her.

"I *am* helping you, Mr. Holloway. And you don't need to pay me."

"Ken," he said, not caring how she addressed him. He watched her in the mirror. She was plain, her dust-colored brown hair drawn severely behind her head into a bun; her face was devoid of makeup. A scar ran across her temple and cheek; another tiny scar laced the bridge of her nose. He wondered how she'd gotten them. With her bulky blue robe and old-fashioned hairstyle he had guessed her to be a few years older than his thirty-two.

She looked up, caught him watching her in the mirror, and blushed. She seemed like someone transplanted out of his grandmother's generation, Ken thought. Mild, gentle—he regretted he had frightened her, but he thanked fortune that she had cooperated. So far. Moments came when she appeared disturbed by him, sometimes fearful of him, and he couldn't really blame her.

She dabbed the disinfectant on a piece of cotton and began to clean the wound gently. She was standing close enough for him to notice the scent of a sweet perfume.

"Look, go ahead and disinfect the cut. I can barely feel what you're doing," he said, thinking she must be terrified of men.

For only a second he felt something cold, then the sensation changed to a stinging heat. "Ow, dammit!"

"You said—"

"I know. Go ahead," he snapped, watching her in the mirror. She shot him one quick look, and there was fire in her eyes. The glance surprised him because she had seemed timid and shy.

"It goes a little bit below your belt. I think you can reach it."

"Dab that stuff on it. I'm not cut to my thigh!" A flicker of annoyance came because he was hurt and had fallen into the hands of a prudish spinster who was probably terrified by the mere presence of a man. He didn't know there were any such creatures still in existence.

"Ow!" He yelped with pain as she poured the liquid into the cut.

Laughing in spite of the sting, realizing his snap judgments about her hadn't been altogether accurate, he turned around and placed his hands on both sides of her, hemming her in. Her cheeks turned pink, and she looked up at him. Suddenly, to his amazement, he was ensnared, held in a spell woven invisibly by wide hazel eyes that were filled with absolute trust and seemed to look into his soul.

As the moment stretched on he was drawn to

her, leaning closer. "Do you always trust every-one?" he asked. Effortlessly she seemed to reach out and touch something deep within him that he always kept closed to others.

"Millie," he said, rolling the name on his tongue. His heart missed a beat as the knowledge sank in that she was a sensuous woman in spite of her shyness, and his curiosity about her soared. "What's your full name? Millicent?"

"Camilla," she whispered, tilting her head back.

"Camilla," he said, and this time he deliberately drew the word out, watching as her green-gold eyes developed a languid coaxing look. He was sure she didn't realize how she was responding to him.

The sound of the police car's motor signaling the officers' departure startled them both and broke the electric tension. She slipped out from under his arm and went into the bedroom. He followed, aware she was flustered by his presence, and amused at how obviously she was avoiding look-ing at his bare chest.

"Don't you want an explanation from me?" he asked in a husky voice, watching her intently. "You're an accessory now."

Two

She blinked in surprise because the idea of being an accessory hadn't crossed her mind.

"Will you listen if I tell you my side of the story?"

"Of course." Her hazel eyes studied him solemnly. "While we talk would you like to have some hot coffee?"

"Yes, thanks. Do you have any whiskey?"

She shook her head, and he sighed. "I didn't think you would. Coffee's fine."

"Let's go to the kitchen."

He pulled on his shirt and buttoned it at the waist as he followed her. In the kitchen the box in the corner caught his eye.

"Where'd the pups come from?"

"I found them abandoned on the highway, and I couldn't just drive by and leave them. I've found homes for three of them already." He rattled the knob of the kitchen door.

She gave him a worried look. "Can the authorities follow your tracks from his house to here?"

"No. I don't think even a dog could follow the tracks. I went through a stream."

Instantly her gaze flew to his feet and for the first time she noticed he was in his socks.

"I dried my socks in your dryer and my shoes are in the utility room. I meandered around before I got in here."

"You left the back door unlocked."

"I got in with a credit card. You have a flimsy lock."

"I know. My dog is at the vet, but when he's home, I don't worry about someone trying to get inside."

Ken sat and watched her work, knowing his steady gaze disturbed her, but he was curious about her.

Her fingers were long, slender, and dainty with short, unpolished nails like a young girl's. He glanced again at the scars on her face and felt a tug of pity for her. The scars had no doubt contributed to her shyness. He wondered what she looked like beneath the robe.

"Where do you work?"

"I'm a dietitian for the city school system. I plan menus for the elementary schools. And I do volunteer work," she said, and picked up a pie. "I can heat this quickly. Would you like some?"

He nodded, his mind on other things. "Where do you do the volunteer work?"

"At the Sunshine Mission in the city."

He watched her through half-closed eyes, thinking about the events of the night and Walter's death.

With quick efficiency she had coffee brewing, and then she sat down to wait. She sat facing him across the table, and again he caught a whiff of her perfume, the scent of roses and apple blossoms.

"You were going to tell me what happened," she said, looking at him with wide, thickly lashed eyes.

"Yeah. I'll try and shorten the story. You have a neighbor who lives down the mountain, Mr. Walter Poplin."

"They say he's a millionaire. Everyone in Strawberry Mountain has heard of him," she said. Ken Holloway gave her a strange, sardonic grin. It disturbed her to have him sit so close with his shirt unbuttoned to the waist leaving his chest exposed, talking to her in the dead of night in his husky voice. He sat back in the chair, one arm hooked over the back, in a relaxed manner, as if it were his kitchen instead of hers. There was an intimacy to the moment that bothered her and made her acutely aware of him. He was handsome enough to be a movie star, she thought.

It was difficult to concentrate on his words and keep her eyes from straying over his face and down across his chest.

When she had attended to his cut, each touch had sent sharp, electric shocks through her, and she had been conscious of his amusement. She felt plain and awkward around him because she had been thrown into a situation where she was out of her depth, having to handle a powerful, commanding, handsome male—a first in her life!

Her gaze drifted down, resting on his chest where his white shirt gaped open, revealing swirls of curly dark hair. Then she realized he had stopped talking. Embarrassed, she looked up to see him watching her with smoldering speculation in his eyes.

"You were saying. . . ?" she prompted, feeling the hot blush that rose to her cheeks.

"What did you last hear?" he asked in a mocking tone.

Amusement at herself momentarily relieved her embarrassment, but it was short-lived. "I'm sorry, my mind wandered. You're a very handsome man."

He blinked and looked startled, his brows arching while he stared at her, and she wondered if he had mistaken her statement for a come-on.

"Go ahead and explain how you're not the man the police want," she said matter-of-factly. "I'll get the pie now. The coffee is ready." She moved away from the table quickly, aware that he was watching her. She glanced over her shoulder to see he had stretched out his long legs, crossed them at the ankles, and had his arms folded over his chest.

"I've been trying to take over his company, Poplin Trucking, and he's fought me all the way. We were about two days from finalizing the deal— Monday morning, to be exact. Unexpectedly he called me and asked me to come meet with him tonight at his house."

She placed a steaming cup of black coffee in front of him along with a slice of hot apple pie she had just removed from the microwave oven. He swiveled around in his chair, leaning close and breathing deeply. "Mmm, that smells good! Did you make it?"

"Yes, as a matter of fact. Care for cream or sugar?" she asked as she sat down across from him.

"No, thanks. Just black," he said. He noticed that her blue robe had little strings popping free from all the washings it must have had. It was thick, lumpy, and shapeless, hiding her figure as well as the winter coat had that she'd been wearing when he had met her. For a moment in the closet he had held her briefly against him, but at that time his nerves were frayed, and his mind had been on the danger of the police. Now he was becoming increasingly curious to see how she looked. He cut into the pale, flaky crust and thick golden apples of the pie. It tasted as good as it looked, and he took another bite. "This is delicious."

"Thanks. I like to cook." He couldn't remember any of the women he had dated ever saying that. He sipped the hot coffee and continued talking. "To tell it briefly: When I got to Poplin's house no one answered my knock, so I pushed the door open and went inside. Someone hit me from behind. When I came to, I found Poplin lying on the floor a few feet away. He'd been shot, and the gun was in my hand."

"The gun you have with you?" she asked.

He nodded and wondered if he would have been better off not to have mentioned it. She finished her narrow wedge of pie and raised her blue china coffee cup to her lips, looking at him expectantly over the rim.

She stared at him as if she didn't believe a word he had said.

"I'm telling you the truth! Help me, and I'll pay you well."

"If I decide you're telling the truth," she said with icy dignity, "I'll continue to hide you, and you won't have to buy my assistance. But if I think you're lying, I'll turn you in the first chance I get," she said.

"Let me tell you something for future reference—don't threaten a real crook that you'll turn him in, because you might goad him into doing something violent."

"Is that a threat, Mr. Holloway?"

Suddenly he grinned. "Ken. You know you remind me of my third-grade teacher, Mrs. Whitaker. She was a stickler for doing things the right way. 'Don't chew gum in class, Kenneth. Don't run into the street after the ball.'"

He tilted his head and studied her, smiling at her. She couldn't resist smiling back, and they both had to laugh. It eased the tension between them, and he continued. "It took me a few minutes to get my bearings—precious time lost," he said, and finished his pie. "Someone had not only shot Poplin but also set the house on fire—although at the moment I regained consciousness, I didn't know the house was on fire."

"Had they tried to kill you by hitting you on the head?"

"No, I don't think so. I think whoever did it intended only to knock me unconscious—and set me up to face a murder rap." Ken hurt all over physically, yet another hurt ran deeper—shock over someone hating him so badly, shock over Walter Poplin's death.

Camilla picked up the coffee cup again, propping her elbows on the table, holding it with the slender fingers of both hands while she sipped. For the first time he noticed two thin scars lacing her left hand. Except for the scars, her skin was porcelain-smooth, flawless.

In the soft light she looked younger, prettier, and he wondered again what had happened to her.

She sat quietly, waiting for him to continue. He wanted to blank the night out of mind, out of his life. He was still having trouble grasping the fact that it had actually happened to him. He knew he would remember every moment in vivid detail as long as he lived—from the acrid smell of gunpowder when he had opened his eyes, to the damp, cloying mist outside, the deep snowdrifts, the soft, wet earth when he had slipped and fallen in his scramble up the mountainside. The first terrible moments of panic when everything seemed beyond his control.

His thoughts came back to the present. He heard the ticking of the clock in the silence of the kitchen and saw only the soft light turned on over the stove and Camilla's wide hazel eyes watching him, waiting for him to finish.

"I think the murderer tipped off the police; I could dimly hear sirens when I regained consciousness. I'll have to admit I was shocked and confused."

"Would you care for more pie?" she asked, rising to refill their coffee cups.

"No, thanks, but that was the best apple pie I've ever eaten," he said sincerely. He was rewarded with a smile that revealed even white teeth and a dimple in her left cheek that he hadn't noticed before.

Camilla looked down at the coffee, swirling it in her cup. Kenneth Holloway seemed to be a man who would remain unperturbed by the most violent circumstances. His story was plausible, but she suspected he was a commanding man accustomed to manipulating people. She had no fear of physical danger, but she knew he might be deceiving her.

Only half believing, she stared at him. "Why don't you go to the police, tell them your story, and ask for their help?"

"Because Walter Poplin helped put the police chief of Strawberry Mountain into his job. Chief Leonard has some tie to Walter or the company, and I don't think it would be wise to trust the police at this point." He stared at her solemnly, as if he were debating something, and she waited quietly.

"Walter Poplin was my father," he said finally.

Shocked, she replied, "Your name is Holloway."

"That's right. I was his illegitimate son, and at the time of my birth he didn't want anything to do with my mother or me," he said flatly, his blue eyes developing a glacial frostiness. "She later married and had children. I have five half brothers and sisters. In the ninth grade I won some awards, and there was an article in the paper about me that caught Walter's attention.

"He spent months having me watched, making

up his mind. Then he came to my mother with a proposition. He'd had three unhappy marriages, one daughter who had died at an early age, and no sons. If I would go to live with him, he'd take me in and raise me as his own and give my mother a pension. My dad couldn't hold a job, and with six kids we were always in need. When they finally told me about the offer from Walter, I agreed to go," he said grimly.

She stared at him, seeing a different man and hearing the unmistakable bitterness in his voice. He had had a trauma in his teen years that was probably as disrupting in its own way as the car accident had been to her, and empathy filled her.

"From the first moment Walter and I were at loggerheads. I suppose I was a headstrong teen who saw the world in black and white. At the time I hated him for what he had done to my mother and me. I hated him for coming back into our lives and taking me away from my family. We were poor, but we were happy and close, and he shut off some of that closeness forever. And it hurt my mother. She still loved him to some degree; I could see that. Anyway, I fought him every step of the way just short of going so far that he would send me back to them and take the money away from Mom.

"After I was grown and on my own, when I became successful in business, I saw the opportunity to buy Walter out, to take over the company he was running, the one thing in life—other than money—that he loved."

Camilla hurt for him and the rejection and bitterness in his past. Remembering the snapshot the police had shown her, she wondered what he was like when he was happy, in the carefree moments. She felt like patting his hand.

"Long ago I refused to do what he wanted in the company. He threatened to disinherit me. I didn't care what he did; I wasn't going to give in to his demands, and I was sure enough of myself to oppose him and leave."

Camilla could easily see that Kenneth Holloway was sure of himself. He had a take-charge attitude about everything, even when he was hurt and in shock. He dominated the room. In a different way than in those first shocking seconds, he frightened her. His piercing blue eyes, his toughness, his overpowering virility, all disturbed her. Yet at the same time she was inexorably drawn to him.

"If you're such a businessman, don't you have your own attorney to call for help?"

"After tonight how do I know whom I can trust?" he asked sharply.

"It seems to me you should be able to trust your own lawyer."

"How many people knew I was going to see Walter tonight? Very damn few, I'll tell you!" he snapped angrily, his face flushing as he clenched his fist.

"Do you trust anyone?" she asked, thinking he had a tough, cynical approach to life.

He glared at her, and she stared calmly back at him.

"I haven't been given much reason in life to trust people. My folks made the arrangement with Walter before I was consulted about it. Trust someone, and you'd better be willing to accept the consequences!"

She was caught between annoyance at such a cynical attitude and regret and sympathy for someone who'd been betrayed by friends and family.

Suddenly his brows arched in amusement. "You look as if you're going to cry."

"No, you don't need my tears," she said dryly, "but I feel sorry for you."

"You feel sorry for me," he repeated softly, thinking it was a first, a unique reaction from a female acquaintance. Never in his life had he had a woman—from his mother to his latest lady—pity him. It was novel and amusing. But he couldn't help feeling a flash of annoyance. He did *not* need her sympathy! And he told her so.

"You don't need to look at me that way and tear up with pity."

Her straight brown eyebrows came together in a momentary frown, then she laughed. "You're right!"

Her laughter was a pleasant sound in the silence. Her dimple showed again, and he found he felt better when she smiled. The electric tension that had sprung to life before happened again. Her breathing altered, and something flickered in the depths of his eyes.

He was the most blatantly sexy man she had ever encountered, Camilla told herself. Sensuality oozed from every handsome pore in his body. He winked at her, and she knew she would be in trouble if she didn't put some kind of wall between them. She was far too vulnerable to yield to the charm of a desperate, worldly man who, under other circumstances, wouldn't have given her a hello or a second glance.

"Care for more coffee?"

"I'll get the coffee." Instantly he reached for the chrome pot, stretching out his arm, making his shirt gap open. While his head was turned her gaze ran across his chest. She held out her cup and watched him fill it, then his own. His expression had changed, and he seemed preoccupied as he picked up his coffee.

"I need to know who stood to gain from my father's murder, as well as who would gain from framing me."

In the distance the high wail of a siren sounded, and they both glanced at the door. When she turned to look at him, his brow was creased in a frown.

"If they remain in the vicinity, I might have to stay tomorrow if you'll let me. Will you have to go to work?"

"I'll let you stay. I'm on vacation for two weeks because of Christmas, but I work tomorrow at the mission."

"Oh, Lordy, Christmas! Damn."

"What religion are you?"

"Protestant. I celebrate Christmas. I just forgot about it in the crisis tonight. My plans will be changed now." He ran his fingers through his hair distractedly. She watched the thick dark locks spring free from his hand while she wondered how he had intended to spend his Christmas.

"Are you going away or having relatives here?" he asked her.

"Neither. I'm staying here and helping at the mission."

"You don't have any family?" he asked, carrying on the conversation while his thoughts were elsewhere.

"No, not this year. I have three married sisters and my parents have retired and moved to Arizona, where Cindy, my oldest sister lives. Since I don't have a husband and children, and they do, we all go to one of their houses for Christmas," she said. "This year Lou, my sister in Atlanta, is having everyone, but I decided to stay home because I can be of real help at the mission."

"You don't mind being alone for Christmas?"

"I won't really be alone if I work at the mission, and no, I don't mind. My folks are involved with their grandchildren, and my sisters are busy with their families. I feel sort of unnecessary sometimes," she said.

"Sounds like my family," he said. "I love my folks and they love me, but we're not really a tightly knit family. I'm pretty close to my brothers and sisters, but our homes are scattered all over the country; we don't try to get together for Christmas. One sister, Jean, lives in Des Moines, where our folks live. Is there anyone coming here tomorrow? Friends, relatives?"

"No. I'll be working at the mission tomorrow afternoon."

"I should be able to get out of here by then."

"Where can you go?"

"I have a condo no one knows about except my mother. If I can get there, I'll be able to investigate people without anyone locating me."

While he was talking, Camilla removed pins from her hair, unfastening the bun at the back of her head.

Ken folded his arms on the table and leaned forward slightly, his concentration on earlier events fading as he watched her. A lock of silky brown hair feel to her waist, and then another. He talked quietly, only a fraction of his attention on his words while she withdrew more pins and was transformed before his eyes, an alchemy that made his pulse skip beats.

"I ran from Walter's house tonight. While I was unconscious someone took my wallet too. I don't have a dime."

"They robbed you?"

"They probably weren't after my money, just some incriminating evidence to leave behind. I'll bet the police find something from from the wallet on the grounds. I ran because I wanted to be free for a while to see what I could discover. When you realize someone hates you enough to go to such lengths, it's jarring."

"I'm sure," she said gently, her voice filled with sympathy.

He barely noticed. Shining brown hair fell across her shoulders, and it changed her appearance drastically. She looked lovely; the scars weren't important. He saw only her wide eyes, her flowing brown hair, her lips that were curved and full.

"You were saying," she prodded, her cheeks becoming pink as she pulled the collar of her robe higher beneath her chin.

He met her gaze steadily, his voice lowering. "I

forgot what I was saying. You're a very beautiful woman."

Instantly her lashes dropped; they were a shadow above her prominent cheeks. "I'll help you. It isn't necessary for you to say things like that," she said softly.

He reached across the table to raise her chin so he could look her in the eye. His finger touched her cheek lightly. "How'd you get the scars?"

"In a car wreck when I was thirteen," she answered in a flat voice.

"Ahh," he said, realizing the disfigurement had occurred at a vulnerable age. He guessed she had simply withdrawn to protect herself.

"My scars don't show," he said with a cynical tone, and she looked into his eyes again.

"Maybe yours are the worst kind," she whispered, "because no one expects them to affect you. Did you shoot Walter Poplin?"

His eyes were deep, royal-blue, the color of a china plate she owned. Nothing flickered in them; he didn't glance away or avoid meeting her steady gaze. "No, I did not. I swear I didn't. I've told you the truth."

The moment became suspended, taut with electricity. Invisible sparks danced like flower petals caught in a windstorm. Her eyes widened and her tongue darted out to lick her lower lip.

His pulse jumped, accelerating in a way he hadn't felt since a teenager. As they looked into each other's eyes his deduction, made hours earlier, reversed.

She wasn't older than he was—with absolute sureness he decided she was much younger. Her eyes, which had seemed hazel, now looked as green as seawater flecked with golden sunlight. Her lips were curved and full and inviting, and his pulse began to hammer in his veins. He tilted her chin up, and she looked at him with a steady, curious, yet compelling expression that made him feel as if he were drowning in her big wide eyes.

"How old are you?"

"Twenty-five," she whispered, her pink tongue touching her lips again.

"I'm thirty-two," he said, as if he had to let her know about himself. Her mouth looked sweeter and more appealing than fine brandy or wine; sweeter, hotter. He had to taste, to touch her, to discover what she would do.

He leaned closer and heard her quick intake of breath. He saw and felt her instant response to nothing more than his mere proximity. Ken was certain she knew little about men; the thought excited him in a way that he wouldn't have believed possible.

During his adult life he hadn't ever wanted to become involved with a virgin, but the pull on his senses was now totally compelling. Leaning across the table, he brushed her lips with his. They were soft like velvet, hinting of hidden promises.

Some small voice in the back of his mind laughed cynically. Shyness, coyness, embarrassment, were all qualities he disliked in his companions, but he felt caught in something beyond his control, some deep attraction she held that fired his imagination and curiosity.

"Camilla," he said in a deep, husky voice, watching her eyes widen, and he realized she was a warm, sensual woman who had never been truly, deeply loved. For a moment he felt a sense of déjà vu, as if she were the woman he had dreamed about, longed for so many times, only to be so disappointed by never finding her that he had stopped hoping or expecting or looking.

As he studied her Camilla was drawn to him like a flower to sunlight. His thickly lashed eyes were intense, compelling, a stormy blue. Her heart thudded violently, hammering loudly enough for both of them to hear.

He pushed away his chair and came around the table, and all she could do was stare at him, transfixed. She was far out of her depth in a situation she had never experienced before, lost to emotions that were new, as powerful as hurricane-force winds.

He took her wrist, tugging gently. "Camilla, stand up," he whispered.

"I shouldn't," she answered.

He reached down to pull her to her feet. Something seemed to explode deep inside her and reverberate through every bone and nerve and pore of her body. She was helpless to stop what they both knew was inevitable.

Three

Ken pulled her to him, his arms circling her waist, as he bent his head to seek her mouth.

His tongue thrust against her soft lips, pushing, moving them apart. He watched as her eyes closed, and then his tongue was in her mouth, tasting intimately, exploring and touching and drowning in a sweetness he couldn't remember encountering in his lifetime.

Her slender arms wrapped around his neck, and she pressed against him. He was stunned. She was neither aggressive nor love-starved, nor was she prudish or shy or coy. She was hungrily taking everything he could give. She was as natural and responsive in his arms as if she had been waiting for him, *only him,* all her life. It was as if this was what she had expected, planned, and known would be her destiny, and his pulse roared with a thunder that was strong enough to drown out all other sounds. He tightened his arms around her.

A wave of longing surged deep within her. She was on fire in a way she had never known, dazzled by this dangerous man, who was far more of a threat to her now than he had been earlier.

His kisses were magic; her senses were stormed. His hand drifted over the curve of her hip and up across her back, and her heart pounded wildly as she clung to him.

He fitted her closer, leaning over her, cupping the back of her head with his hand while he kissed her passionately.

Finally he shifted to look down at her. Her expression was sultry; her lips rosy from his kiss. There was a longing in her eyes that made him ache.

She was so close to him, she could see every detail of the stubble of dark beard on his jaw, the fine, tanned skin, his thick, black lashes, and unruly wavy hair. Trying to summon back reason, she moved away, pulling the robe around her tightly, shaking her hair behind her head.

Ken leaned one hip against the counter, and put his hand on his other hip. He watched her with a bemused, curious, smoldering stare. He was virile, handsome, blatantly masculine and, she reminded herself, he would go out of her life as abruptly as he had come into it.

"Are you married?" she asked, unable to resist inquiring.

"No," he answered, smiling at her; he didn't need to ask if there was a man in her life, because he knew there wasn't and most likely hadn't been.

She seemed totally vulnerable, almost delicate physically, until he kissed her. Then she was an earthy woman—fiery, natural, and instantly responsive.

He shifted his thoughts back to the problem at hand to keep from reaching for her again. "Camilla, there's something else I didn't tell you. I know the murderer intended to kill him, but Walter was alive when I regained consciousness. As I bent over him he whispered to me."

"Did he say who'd done it?"

"No, and not everything he said to me makes sense. I couldn't understand every word. What I remember is: ' . . . knew you would be here . . . framed . . . set up because the money . . . knew everything . . . it was more than . . . wanted all. . . .' "

"Why didn't you tell me that earlier?" she asked, astounded that he would keep such important information from her.

"I thought it might sound fishy to you until you knew my whole story."

"I believed you."

He reached out to caress her cheek. "You're so damn trusting. Aren't you constantly disappointed?"

She shrugged. "Occasionally, but mostly no. People are good."

He gave her a cynical, mocking smile that stirred feelings of pity and regret inside her again.

"There you go, feeling sorry for me," he said with amusement. "I can see it in your eyes." He leaned close. "I *don't* need your sympathy. I have a good life," he said, wondering why he felt the need to defend his life-style when he'd never needed to before. "I travel, I own successful businesses, and am on the verge of getting another one. I was exceptionally lucky with land that had oil leases during the oil boom. I ski, swim, hunt, and play tennis, and have other hobbies that entertain me. I know some fascinating people."

"Are you trying to convince me or yourself?" she asked quietly. "What do you do when you need someone?"

"I have friends, my lawyers, women I've known, engineers—" He broke off suddenly, his eyes narrowing as a cold shock hit him. Tonight he was in the worst jam of his life—something beyond his control—and he couldn't turn to one of the people he had listed and trust him or her without a qualm.

He blinked as he stared at Camilla and she moved away. He watched her work, enjoying following the quick efficient movements of her hands as she rinsed the coffee cups and put away the pie. He observed without realizing he was staring, because his thoughts were still on the startling discovery that he didn't have quite the kind of friends and colleagues and women he'd always thought he had.

"My sisters and brothers would help me," he said.

Camilla turned, momentarily puzzled, then she nodded her head. "You're still thinking about people you could go to in a crisis. You don't have to prove to me you have friends. I know the women in your life would help you." She gave him a merry smile. "They'd probably do whatever you wanted."

He felt as if he had stepped on a burr. "Don't be so cheerful about the women in my life!"

"Why not?" She paused to dry her hands on a fluffy yellow towel.

He arched his brow and relaxed a fraction. "Don't sound so eager to toss me back to them and out of your life."

He forgot his worries and crossed the room to put his hands on both sides of her, hemming her in against the counter. He leaned down so they were at eye level. Her cheeks became pink, but she watched him with a playful curiosity in her expression.

"That's where you belong," she said. "Remember? We're worlds apart, and we always will be. I don't belong in your world, not for one minute. Now, do you want to sleep on the sofa?"

"Do you really think that I'll go on my way and never call or see you again after the kisses we've shared?"

Her merriment faded, and her brows drew closer in a slight frown. "Please . . . will you step out of my way?" she said, finding it difficult to talk.

"I want to take you out to dinner when I can."

Her frown increased, giving him a little pinch of dismay. "We'll see when the time comes," she said stiffly, and he knew she had no intention of dating him. He always had had more than reasonable success with women, and suddenly he felt at a loss with Camilla Blake. "I'm not very adept at flirting."

He caught her chin in his hand, and all his laughter fled. "Say *Ken*. I have yet to hear you say my name."

Her eyes were like emeralds with chips of gold, changing as he watched her.

"Ken," she said softly. She was as tempting as a bright flame on a cold night, yet he knew he could hurt her so easily. Vulnerable where men were concerned, she was not a woman for a brief affair. And he was not a man for a lasting commitment. He had too many plans, too much he wanted to do before he settled into family life. He moved away from her, jamming his hand into his pocket, momentarily torn by conflicting emotions. He was drawn to her like a moth to a flame. She had helped him, trusted him completely—and he didn't want to repay her trust by hurting her.

He walked restlessly around the room, stopping to pull the window shade a fraction away from the window to look outside. Mist hung over the ground, thicker than before; the visibility was zero. Somewhere out there policemen were searching for him. And somewhere in the city was the man who had committed the crime. Ken ran his fingers through his hair as he mulled over his problems.

"Tomorrow morning I'll slip out of here, and no one will ever know we've crossed paths."

She drew a sharp breath, hating to hear him talk about leaving.

"Camilla." He said her name in a sexy drawl that sparked her nerves and summoned her full attention. He smiled at her, the creases in his cheeks and at the corners of his eyes making him even more handsome. "When I talked about slipping away from here, I didn't mean we wouldn't see each other again."

Had her expression shown her feelings that

clearly? she wondered, disturbed that he could guess her thoughts so effortlessly. She nodded her head. "Do you want to sleep on the sofa?" she asked him for the second time.

"I don't think I'll sleep anywhere tonight," he snapped. He waved his hand. "You go to bed. Thanks for the coffee and pie and the offer of the sofa."

"Would you like to talk some more? Maybe go back over everything you remember. You might think of something else that was important."

He gave her a speculative look and then smiled. "That's a good idea. You don't mind staying up?"

She shook her head. "I'm not exactly drowsy either," she answered lightly, thinking that was the understatement of a lifetime. Her lips still tingled from his kisses, and her heart skipped as she watched him. He was a wonder to her in every way—the handsome, charming man she had met early in the evening, the warm human being she was discovering now, the incredibly sexy man who had just kissed her.

The world outside was quiet in the silence of the dead of night, adding more intimacy to the moment and their time together. They talked in softened voices with the light turned down low, and she felt bound to him in a way that transcended time and place.

"I'm sorry I frightened you at first," he said. "I knew you were in the room, and I knew you'd open the closet. But when I hid, I didn't know if you'd bring someone home with you or not. Then there never seemed to be a good moment to step out and announce my presence."

"Want me to put another pot of coffee on? It won't take a minute."

"Sit down, I'll do it." He took the pot from her and worked quickly. His strong fingers were long, the nails clipped short, and his gold watch glinted in the dim light. He had, Camilla noticed, rolled his shirtsleeves up, revealing his wrists and the short dark hairs on his arms.

"Want to sit in the living room?" she asked. "It'll be more comfortable. I can plug the coffee maker in there."

"Sure."

He carried the coffeepot and she carried the mugs. She switched on the twinkling lights of the Christmas tree. The room smelled invitingly of pine, and the multicolored bulbs gave off a bright enough glow for them to see to get around the room. Packages were piled under the tree, and he was glad to see so many because it meant she had family and friends whom cared about her. During the first hour or so they'd spent together there had seemed something forlorn about her that made him feel protective toward her even though he had known her only a brief time. But the more he got to know Camilla, the less he thought she needed anyone's protection. She seemed contented, possessing an inner satisfaction that he envied.

His defense of his life-style still bothered him. Why had he had to defend himself to her? He was the one with the full life, a busy schedule, Christmas parties he could have attended if he planned to stay in the States, the vacation in Switzerland with Sheryl, while Camilla was alone and intended to stay alone. Yet when he had looked closely at his life, he had been surprised. The crisis seemed to reveal things he had never noticed before. Maybe his life wasn't as full and satisfying as he had thought. Maybe that was why he was also so restless.

Ken touched an ornament, a fragile German glass bird with a spun glass tail that he could have shattered with the slightest squeeze of his fingers.

"This looks old."

"It is. We had some of these when I was a kid. Mom got tired of them and wanted all new ornaments and told all of us to take what we'd like. My sisters didn't want them either, but I like old things."

He smiled at her, pleased because he liked old things too. Then he went back to studying the tree. Next he walked around the room looking at family pictures, the old-fashioned mahogany furniture, the beige antique-silk drapes that were pulled shut, seascapes done in watercolors and oils.

"You like the ocean?"

"I've only seen the sea a couple of times, but I love it."

He moved on, looking at the bookcase that filled one wall beside the fireplace. He pulled out a book and glanced questioningly at her. "You like movies too?"

"Yes, movies and castles. Castles are fascinating. At least what I've read about them in books is fascinating. I haven't actually been in a castle."

He shoved the book back into place and picked up a snapshot of her family from the marble-topped table. He gave her a quick glance. "These are your sisters?"

"Yes."

"They're beautiful," he said, something Camilla had heard all her life. "You're quite a bit younger, aren't you?" Ken asked, curious about her family.

"Yes. Lou is the closest to me in age. She's nine years older than I am—she's thirty-four."

He wondered if having beautiful sisters had added to Camilla's shyness over her scars.

"How about a fire?" he asked, and she nodded. In minutes logs were blazing and crackling in the slate fireplace. The room took on a cozy warmth, and Camilla settled on the sofa, doubling her legs beneath her. Deep contentment settled over her, and it came from doing nothing more than watching him.

Ken sat on the other end of the rose-and-gold–striped sofa, folding his arms across his chest and stretching his long legs out on the marble-topped coffee table.

"I've been thinking about what I'll do," he said quietly. "If I can get out of here, I can go to my condo. I can have absolute peace and quiet there. My lawyers don't know about it, my lady friends—"

He paused, reaching to take her hand. "I'm sorry."

"Don't be ridiculous!" she said, smiling at him. "I know you have women in your life. It would be absurd for you to tell me you didn't. You've kissed me. Kisses aren't promises."

He couldn't resist. He leaned forward to tilt her face up. "They're not, Camilla Blake? You may be surprised someday."

She blushed, and he felt something warm and good inside. He wanted to pull her onto his lap, but he held back.

"You were saying you could go to your condo."

"Yeah. I escape from everyone there. If I can get out of your house, off this mountain, and out of Strawberry Mountain, I can hole up at my place, hire a detective." He leaned back and closed his eyes.

He was quiet so long, she finally asked softly, "Are you going to sleep?"

"No. I can't stop worrying about Walter's death. I was thinking about what happened. After you gave me my wallet back at the club parking lot, I drove to my hotel. I ate dinner downstairs in the hotel restaurant with a business acquaintance. We separated about half past eight."

She watched him while he talked, her gaze roaming over him freely because his eyes were closed. His black lashes were thick above his cheeks. His prominent cheekbones and strong jaw were softened by the cap of wavy black hair; his mouth was well shaped, full enough to be sensual yet still masculine. Her gaze trailed lower over his muscular chest, his thin waist, and long legs. She wondered about the women in his life, curious if there was one special woman.

"When I got back to my apartment, the phone was ringing. It was Walter, and he said it was urgent that I come out to see him tonight. Now, there's a funny thing." He opened his eyes and turned his head to look at her. "I'd planned on flying out of here if the fog lifted enough. A lot of people knew I had originally planned to leave here this evening. No one knew fog would set in and I'd be here, which makes this seem unplanned."

"I think the airport shut down rather early this afternoon."

"It did, but I'm flying my own plane." Frowning, he sat up and glanced at his watch. "Damn, I'd like to make a phone call."

"Go ahead."

"Nope. It's long-distance, and I don't want anything to tie you to me. I'll slip out in the morning, and no one will know our paths crossed."

She wondered if he wanted to call the woman or women he dated. And another thought occurred to her. "Go ahead and call if you have a friend who's worried about you. Won't your parents be worried?"

"My dad's no longer living. And now Walter's gone too. I don't need to call Mom yet. She'll know I'm all right; she rolls with the punches. And my friends can wait," he said grimly, thinking about Sheryl. He knew he couldn't have talked as freely to her as he had to Camilla.

He ran his fingers through his hair, then leaned forward with his hands on his knees. The coffee was done and Camilla poured two cups, then sat down in front of the fire, shaking her hair away from her face, her back to the hearth.

"I didn't want to go to his house. Every time Walter and I are together, we get on each other's nerves and end up in an argument. At first I refused, but he seemed to want to see me so badly, I agreed to go at half past nine."

"That's about the time I was leaving Tonio's Restaurant with a friend."

"Someone who was at the cocktail party?" Ken asked, curious, wondering if he had been mistaken and she did have a man in her life.

"Yes, Claire Ramsey. She's president of Friends of the Library. Go ahead. I didn't mean to interrupt."

He was glad she had. His thoughts had been so intent on earlier events, he had watched Camilla without thinking about how much he was drawn to her. The interruption changed his thoughts, and now they were fully on her. She looked enticing seated in front of the fire with her brown hair cascading over her shoulders and her long, slender legs tucked under her. He wanted to sit down beside her and pull her into his arms and kiss her, but he curbed the impulse and tried to shift back to the problems at hand.

"I drove to Walter's. Since he was expecting me, he had turned off the alarm equipment that would have alerted him to someone driving up to the house. The door opened a few inches when I knocked on it. I thought he might have stepped outside. I looked around and called to him, but no one answered, and the dogs didn't appear. I didn't give it that much thought, because sometimes the dogs are penned in the backyard.

"Finally I pushed open the door and went inside. The hall was dark, but I remember when I approached the house, I saw lights shining in all the windows. I went inside and walked about twenty feet. No one answered my calls, and I stopped. By this time I was beginning to wonder what was going on. I heard a shuffle," he said with surprise, sitting up straighter.

"I remember that I heard someone come up behind me. I'd forgotten until right now. I started to turn and something struck my head. Pain blotted out everything, and I didn't see anything else until I regained consciousness. The lights were blazing then." He rubbed his forehead, trying to remember every detail possible. Even though she knew he could be deceiving her, she believed he was telling her the truth. His voice was deep, the only sound except for the occasional clink of a coffee cup on a saucer or the crackling of the fire. His words came slowly, as if he were lost in memories, and she wondered how deeply the trauma of tonight would affect him.

"I was so groggy. I stood up and staggered back to the front door. It was locked, bolted from the inside. The alarm was going off then. I turned around to go back into the room. I wanted to call to Walter, but I couldn't because I was still fuzzy from the blow. I heard a groan. Walter was sprawled on the floor on his stomach. I knelt beside him and saw the pool of blood. He whispered my name. I rolled him over and felt his pulse. It was weak and erratic, but he was still alive. I ran to call an ambulance. The phone was dead; probably the lines had been cut by the murderer."

Aware of how terrifying it must be in such a situation, Camilla hurt for Ken. She took another drink of the hot, black coffee, her attention still on him.

"I went back to Walter, and he caught my coat to pull me closer. I couldn't hear or understand everything he said. I told you what I think he said. Then he stopped breathing. When I heard sirens, I picked up the pistol and ran. My car keys were gone. I don't know if someone took them and dropped them in the house or if someone still has them. I felt my pockets and realized my wallet was gone too. I started to go back in the house to hunt for them, but the sirens were getting louder, so I ran through the backyard and climbed the mountain. As I fled I saw the house was on fire. While I watched, flames burst through the roof and windows of the west wing.

"I roamed around the area, climbing higher, wading through a creek. I saw your mailbox and remembered the address." He stood up and carried his coffee cup to the hearth to refill it, then he sat down on the floor facing her.

When he reached out and caught a lock of her hair, she drew in her breath sharply and gave him a solemn look. "First I rang the doorbell. When I realized you weren't home, I went around to the kitchen door. It was easy to get into your house. You ought to get a new lock, dog or no dog. It was only maybe five or ten minutes until I heard your car."

His voice lowered while he talked; his words slowed; he leaned forward slightly, one arm propped on his bent knee. Her hair was silk across his fingers—soft, smooth, sliding over his palm like a caress as he tugged his fingers through it.

"Thanks for letting me stay."

She nodded, looking at him thoughtfully. "Do you have any idea who might have done it?"

Again his thoughts shifted, and he dropped the strand of hair, turning to lean against a chair and stretch his legs out beside her. "Nope. I've been over it a few times, but I can't come up with anyone. I have enemies, I know that. They're only business competitors though. We have clashes over deals, nothing severe enough for this."

"Who stands to gain from this?"

He felt a swift stab of pleasure that she went straight to what he considered the most important point. "When I can give you the answer to your question, I'll probably have the name of the man who's responsible. The first place to check is to see who will stand to inherit from Walter. He cut me out of his will years ago when I walked out of Poplin Trucking. He was a ruthless man who didn't mind cutting corners to get what he wanted. That isn't the way I do business. I've made some business enemies, but some of those same men are friendly when we meet socially. And there can be only a few people who would benefit from both Walter's death and my arrest."

"You say few. Do you have any ideas?"

He shrugged, running the possible suspects through his mind.

"Want to hear some more history about me and my family?"

"Sure, go ahead." Her dimple showed, and he wanted to reach for her, an urge that seemed to come with increasing frequency. A log tumbled and fell in the fireplace, sending a shower of fiery orange sparks dancing up the black chimney. The odor of burning pine mingled with the smell of the freshly cut Christmas tree, and he was glad to be with her in her house. It soothed his taut nerves.

"When I resigned from Poplin Trucking, Walter

was enraged. He said he would disinherit me, stop the pension to Mom, and try to keep me from getting a job elsewhere. I suspected that was what he might do, and I'd been quietly preparing for it long before I quit. I knew I wanted out of his firm. I had money saved and I thought I'd buy another trucking company because I knew the business. Instead, I found an opportunity in the asphalt business that looked too good to pass up. My first plant was in Kansas City; I have a home there. Then I bought land in Texas and was very lucky during the oil boom with the leases I got. After that I bought an asphalt firm in Dallas, where I have a small condo."

The extent of his businesses startled her. He seemed too young to have accomplished so much. She was warm from the fire, relaxed, and very interested in his life. Without thinking, she stretched out on her side on the floor, propping her head up with her hand. He shifted his legs out of her way, and her glance ran swiftly down the length of him.

"Walter tried to ruin me," he said matter-of-factly.

"How terrible!" she exclaimed, unable to keep from interrupting his narrative, seeing how Ken could have become cynical and tough.

"I was enraged, and I've been angry with him all along"—Ken turned clear blue eyes on her—"until this weekend. Now I don't feel any animosity toward Walter," he said, realizing how easy it was to confide his deepest emotions and fears to her.

"You're easy to talk to," he said.

"I'm interested and glad to listen."

"And you don't mind hearing about my problems?"

"Of course not," she said sincerely.

He stared at the fire, his thoughts elsewhere. "Sometimes I think women just want a macho man and a strong shoulder to lean on."

"Not this woman," she replied, and his attention shifted back to her. Her eyes were enormous as she gave him a level look.

"I would rather have one understanding man for a friend than all the macho men in the world, someone who can listen, who cares."

Her words touched him. She was like a treasure found by accident: unique, precious, more important because it was discovered unexpectedly. His chest hurt with a need for her that went far beyond lust.

He was still in shock over the night's events, his emotions still in a turmoil, and he found Camilla a shelter in the storm. He didn't want to say good-bye to her. The knowledge was as clear as a summer sunrise and as firm as the floor beneath him, and it added to the upheaval of the night.

He wanted to know her, to love her, to share his fears and problems and hopes and joys with her. The realization was as jolting as the other shocks he had received earlier. He was honest enough to face his own feelings and he knew, because he'd never felt this way before, that the depth of his need for her meant he might be falling swiftly into a love that would entail absolute commitment.

He stared at her, thoughts whirling in his head. She looked lovely, appealing, serene, as if she were waiting patiently for him while he wrestled with his emotions. He wiggled his feet in front of the fire.

"Why don't you go on?" she prompted quietly.

"In spite of Walter I began to get better and better contracts," Ken said. "I found another asphalt company for sale in Dallas and bought it. Walter didn't hurt me financially, but I was angry with him over what he'd tried to do. We fought openly and publicly, so there are plenty of people who might accept that I'm the guilty party tonight. This past fall an opportunity came up to take over Poplin Trucking, and I decided to go ahead and do it, to get revenge on Walter," he said flatly, noticing Camilla's quick frown. "You think I'm a monster, but I was that angry with him. Now it seems like something that happened a long time ago."

"Your anger?"

"Yes," he said, thinking about the events of the night. "I'm not sure I'll look at anything the same way again."

She reached out to touch his hand in a comforting, reassuring manner that made him focus totally on her. He could see the sympathy in her expression. "You look like you're about to cry over me again," he said lightly, and stretched out facing her, his head propped on his hand. "Sleepy?"

"A little," she said softly. "Go ahead and tell me whatever you started to say about Walter Poplin. It's been in all the papers that you'll succeed in the takeover."

"Yeah, but then I found out Walter had a malignancy, and he wasn't given a good prognosis. He's the kind of man who always wanted to be in control. I guessed without investigating that he was behind everything; he wanted me to take over his business. He knew under the right circumstances I would do it. When I discovered how he had manipulated me, I balked and decided to reconsider the move. We hadn't talked to each other since I found out about his illness, and I think that's what he wanted to talk with me about when he called me." He leaned back against a chair. "There's only one reason I can think of that someone would want both of us out of the way."

"What's that?" she said, curious.

"If he did disinherit me years ago—and I'm sure he did—and made someone else beneficiary, someone he trusted and liked, now with his illness, he may have had a change of heart. He may have planned to change his will. If that person found out about it, there's the motive. And it's the only one I can find."

She sat up to face him, crossing her legs and tucking her robe around them. "If he made someone else beneficiary when you left the company, you should have a good idea who it is."

"I've been thinking about that all night. It would have to be someone who knows the company, who is quite a bit younger than Walter, who would do what he wanted, and is high up in the company. It's been six years since I worked there, but at that time there were about four men who could be candidates. Walter had two supervisors, one for marketing, the other for transportation. They're John Edwards and Bob Jensen. They've both been promoted to vice-presidents. Then there is the senior vice-president and chief accountant, Alan

Moreland. There was a product supervisor, Garland Vickers. Any of the four could be the new beneficiary. And the murderer."

"Did you get along with them when you worked there?"

"Yes, and I remember working with each of them. Garland Vickers is a stickler for rules. Bob Jensen is as ruthless as Walter, and I'm sure he's contributed a great deal to building the company. Alan Moreland is ruthless too, but he has more finesse. He's shrewder. John Edwards is a whiz with numbers. All four are cold, hard businessmen when they want to be."

"Cold enough to murder?"

He looked into her wide hazel eyes. "The possibility of inheriting Walter's estate might change the kindest of hearts."

"Even mine?" she asked lightly. Her eyes sparkled, and he forgot all his problems. With a swift movement he shifted down on the floor beside her, draping his arm over her waist.

"Of course not," he said, seeing the change come over her expression. Her eyes half closed in a lazy, heated look that seemed to draw him closer through an invisible pull.

"I didn't mean to distract you," she said breathlessly.

"Oh, yes, you did!" he teased, feeling ridiculously glad.

Her lashes fluttered, but she gazed at him steadily. "Well, maybe a little," she said in the same breathless voice, and he couldn't resist leaning forward to brush her lips with his.

Her lips parted beneath his, and his light kiss

changed to a passionate one, one that made his body react instantly

As his arm tightened around her he leaned forward. His chest pressed against her breasts as he rolled her over on her back. His arousal was swift and intense, and he wanted to reach for the zipper to her robe. But when she turned her head a fraction and pushed against him he shifted away, sitting up and stretching, flexing his muscles.

Camilla stood up to get more coffee. Her cheeks were flushed as she knelt back down on the floor and refilled their cups. "Go on with your story. You won't get a solution this way."

"No, but this is more fun."

She wrinkled her nose at him playfully, and he was gratified to see that she no longer seemed so self-conscious.

"Those four men might have stood to gain, but I can't imagine any one of them committing a crime of this magnitude," he said thoughtfully. "Three of them are married now. Bob is divorced. I can't see any of them doing this. Yet it wasn't accidental. It was someone who knew Walter and me. It was deliberate, premeditated, carefully planned and executed—and damned if I know who could have done it!"

"If it is one of those men, would your own lawyer be involved too?"

He ran his fingers through his hair. "I don't think so, but then I never would have thought this could happen."

They both paused when they heard a car approaching. They stopped talking to listen, and Camilla became tense, knowing it had to be the police. The car stopped, and in minutes a spotlight played across the front window.

"They're checking on your house to see if everything looks okay," he said quietly. "They're still hunting for me. Camilla, I won't ever forget what you've done for me."

"I won't ever forget either," she said, and her voice was breathless. He watched her as flames flickered and danced and gave orange glints to her hair, throwing her cheeks into shadows, highlighting her straight nose. She leaned back against the sofa and closed her eyes. He wanted to reach for her again.

"What will you do tomorrow?"

"I'll leave, take a circuitous route out of Strawberry Mountain, and go to my condo."

"I hope that condo is close. You may have your picture on the front page of the paper, and someone may recognize you."

"The murder may have happened too late to get in the morning paper."

Her words had slowed, and he realized she was sleepy. He looked at his watch and saw it was five o'clock. It would soon be dawn. Dawn and reality. He watched Camilla until he saw she was asleep.

In sleep she seemed defenseless. And so absolutely trusting. He studied her, taking in each feature while he mentally peeled away the lumpy robe. He realized that her skin, where it wasn't scarred, was flawless and as fine as porcelain. The marks were immaterial to him. She was breathtakingly appealing, and he wondered if it was the shock of the evening that had made him feel that way, if under normal circumstances he would feel the same toward her.

He wanted to take her in his arms and kiss her, to unzip the robe and slip his arms around her. He got up and quietly went to the bedroom to turn down the bed, then he returned to scoop her up in his arms.

Big hazel eyes stared at him as she woke up at once. For a moment she looked startled, then she smiled and wrapped one arm around his neck.

"Damn, you're trusting!" he said.

"What do you intend to do?"

"Carry you to bed because you fell asleep."

"And why shouldn't I trust you when you're doing something nice?"

"Until you asked, you had no way of knowing what I intended."

She smiled at him, tightening her arm around his neck, and she kissed his cheek. "I knew. If you had intended something bad, you would have done it before now. You're a fine person, Kenneth Holloway. So fine," she whispered with a satisfied drowsiness.

Putting his knee on the mattress, he lowered her gently, and then he placed his hands on either side of her to support himself. He ached to lower his weight over her, wanting her badly.

"I'm not a saint!" he admitted. "If you only knew . . ." His body was hard with desire, and he hurt from wanting her so much. He stood up abruptly. "Good night."

"Ken."

His heart missed a beat. "Yes?"

"There are blankets in the hall closet and some extra pillows."

"Yeah, sure," he said, surprised at the surliness in his voice. He jammed his hands in his pockets to keep from touching her. With long strides he crossed the room and left.

Camilla watched him go. She knew he had wanted to kiss her. She had wanted him to, but she fought the impulse to reach up and pull him down. She stood up and pulled off her robe, tossing it over the foot of the bed before slipping beneath the covers.

More than an hour later she opened her eyes to see a hard, muscular arm by her face. She looked up at Kenneth Holloway, who was frowning fiercely as his hand clamped around her waist.

Four

Ken leaned down at the same time she heard the knock on the door.

"The police are here. I didn't want to startle you," he said quietly. "Keep them from coming in, but you have to answer the door."

Startled, momentarily frightened by his frown, she blinked at him, trying to come fully awake.

"Camilla? I'm sorry. I frightened you," Ken said gently, his tight hold on her waist loosening immediately. "Damn, I'm sorry."

Her gaze roamed freely over him, and her breath caught and stopped as abruptly as if she had received a blow to her middle.

He was barechested, his hair unruly, the black strands beaded with moisture, as if he had been in the shower. He was incredibly handsome, and she couldn't stop gazing at him.

She knew in her heart that the only attraction she held for him was as a way to safety. She wasn't beautiful or cosmopolitan or sexy—or anything else that would entice a man like him. Yet whatever his reasons, she couldn't stop what she was feeling for him.

"Camilla?"

She smiled at him. "I'm okay. I'll go to the door."

He stepped back, waiting. She realized he wanted to see her without the robe. She hesitated and then her cheeks became pink as she swung her legs out of the bed. Her gown billowed around her. The nightgown was pink flannel; soft, faded from washings, and unbuttoned at the neck.

Ken watched, his pulse drumming as the gown swept against her figure, outlining the fullness of her breasts, nipping in at her waist, curving over her hips.

"You're staring!" she accused lightly.

All the glib replies he usually was so adept at vanished from his mind. He was fighting to control the ever-present urge to take her in his arms, and there wasn't anything he could think of to say. He turned abruptly and walked away from her.

"See what they want," he said over his shoulder.

Startled by his curtness, she stared at his back, deciding he was gruff because he was worried about the police. She hurried past him to open the front door.

"Morning, ma'am. I'm Officer Collins with the Strawberry Mountain Police. Here's your morning paper."

"Thanks," she said, taking the rolled-up paper from him.

"We're checking houses this morning. Have you seen any strangers in the area?"

"No, I haven't," she said, thinking Ken Holloway was far from a stranger now.

"Do you mind if we look around the yard?"

"No, of course not."

"We're keeping roadblocks up and we've cordoned off this area, but until we apprehend the suspect, be careful. He's armed and considered dangerous. We don't think he can escape from the area without drawing attention to himself."

"Thanks. I'll be very careful."

He turned away, and she closed the door, locking it before returning to the living room. Ken was standing by a window, holding the drape away a fraction to watch the officer leave. He wore his white shirt tucked into the charcoal slacks.

"Thanks again," he said softly, turning to look at her, remembering exactly how she had looked without the robe. "I have to get out of here," he said.

"I don't think you can yet. It sounds as if they have all the roads blocked. With the snow they can pick up your footprints easily."

"I know, but as soon as I eat, I'll try to slip out of here. I'll be careful."

She frowned, thinking about the lawmen and the roadblocks, mentally picturing Ken being chased, or worse, shot by mistake.

"Let me drive down the road to the grocery store to see where the roadblocks are and what your chances are on foot, then I'll come back and we can formulate a plan."

He thought about her idea for a moment. He wasn't accustomed to placing his life and future in the hands of another person. Following her suggestion could work against him, he realized. On the one hand it was a tempting offer, but on the other, possibly a ploy to deceive him.

As she waited for him to speak his gaze focused on her face, still rosy from sleep; her thick mane of brown hair, tangled invitingly; her wide eyes, full of sincerity. He had trusted her before, and he was still willing to trust her completely.

He nodded his head. "That sounds like a fine idea," he said cautiously. "Are you sure you want to? Remember, if you're caught, you'll be considered an accessory."

Camilla was so obviously and enormously pleased that he decided to trust her, he had another battle with himself to keep from reaching for her.

"I want to," she said quietly. "I'll go dress now."

"Breakfast is waiting, sleepyhead."

She smiled and her dimple showed. "I do sleep soundly."

"Wait a minute. Let's see if the murder made the paper."

She unfolded the paper. Dark letters in a small square on the front page seemed to leap up at her.

"It was too late for anything more than a bulletin in this issue." He read aloud, standing pressed close to her side, their heads bent together. "*Bulletin:* Wealthy executive found slain. Around nine P.M. the body of Walter Poplin, owner of Poplin Trucking, was found in his burning home in Strawberry Mountain. He had been shot once through the heart. A suspect, his son Kenneth T. Holloway, allegedly was the last person to see him only moments before the police arrived on the scene."

"Tomorrow I'll be headlines," he said so bitterly, she turned to hug him.

Her hug was spontaneous, catching him off guard. His arms tightened around her instantly, and he closed his eyes, relishing the sensation of holding her and forgetting all his problems. "Are you going to cry over me too?" he whispered in her ear.

She laughed shakily. "I might."

"Don't. I intend to get to the bottom of this. I'll find out who shot Walter."

She took a deep breath and looked up at him with wide eyes.

His feelings for her continued to surprise him. In spite of her initial shyness and self-consciousness, as he had gotten to know her she seemed contented, confident. The realization jarred his thinking. Camilla was self-assured in a way that would carry her through every crisis. He smiled at her as she stepped out of his arms.

"I'll dress," she said, and hurried to the bedroom. Camilla hummed softly to herself. He was going to trust her. She believed what he had said earlier about not trusting others, yet he was trusting her. It generated a strange mixture of emotions in her, both pleasure and amazement.

Ken was in the kitchen when he heard the snap of a window shade. He rushed to the bedroom and saw her raising another shade.

"Dammit, leave them closed!" he said, grabbing her wrist lightly.

She swung around, startled, but not frightened. "They won't see you unless you stand right at the window, and it'll look more suspicious for everything to be closed. I was only going to open . . . some . . ."

She had started out calmly talking to him, but he was standing only inches away, the top buttons of his shirt unfastened, and as she looked at his chest, his mouth, and finally up into his eyes, he saw a change come over her and knew her mind was only on him.

He leaned down, slipping his arms around her, and kissed her, finding her mouth sweet, her kisses fiery.

Abruptly he turned away, making his voice normal as he said, "I suppose you're right about the shades. Go ahead and open them." He rubbed his bristly jaw. "Do you have any disposable razors?"

"Sure. On the shelf in the bathroom cabinet. While I get my things together you shave, and then I'll get a turn in the bathroom to shower and dress."

After he closed the bathroom door, he stood wondering. Was it the trauma of the murder that had drawn him to her? He didn't think it was, but until circumstances were back to normal, he wouldn't know. He wanted her more than he had ever desired a woman. A very basic need tore at him.

He was a worldly, cosmopolitan man, and she was naive, living in her own small world. He shouldn't have had a moment's interest in her, but he did.

As he lathered his face he tried to analyze why. Thinking about her, he had to acknowledge her sensuality touched a chord in him that made him desire her intensely. He stared at his image in the mirror, looking at his cuts and bruises, wondering what Camilla would be like in bed, and suspecting she would fulfill all the promises given in her kisses.

She was helping him to elude the authorities. He couldn't ask for more than that. "Leave her alone!" He ground out the words as if he were trying to convince someone other than himself.

"Ken?"

He heard her soft inquiry through the door. Washing lather off his jaw and drying his face swiftly, he opened the door.

She stared at him with curiosity. "Did you say something to me?"

All he could think about was that she was unique, and he wanted to kiss her.

His desire must have shown in his features. Her eyes flickered, and her expression changed. She became sultry, sleepy-eyed. The transformation was subtle, but as evident as her uneven breathing. He was drawn to her like a puppet with no will of its own.

He dropped the towel negligently on the sink and moved closer, reaching out to pull down the zipper of her robe.

"Ken," she whispered. He had no idea if she had meant the word as a protest or an invitation, but she didn't resist or move away. He opened the robe and slipped his arm around her, fitting her to him, reveling in the feel of her narrow waist, her warm skin through the thin layer of flannel, her soft breast pressing against his arm.

"I don't want to let you go," he said, and was shocked to realize he meant it. "If we're together for two seconds, I want to touch you."

His blood thundered in his veins as he bent his head and covered her mouth with his own. She was soft, sweet, hot. There was a promise given in each kiss that made him want more and more. All his good intentions to leave her alone until things were normal evaporated, and a tremor shook him as he slipped his hand over her rib cage to her full breast.

She gasped, clinging to him, trembling in his arms until he was on fire with need, his body hard and ready, eager to love her.

She seemed to melt in his arms, to quiver and burn like a flame. He wanted to rip away the gown and touch her flesh. He watched her through narrowed eyes, wondering when she would stop him, unable to stop himself. His hand slipped into the open neck of her gown, and his fingers brushed warm, smooth flesh, finding her hard nipple and caressing it with his thumb. He watched her instant reaction as she gasped, and her hips thrust against him.

Suddenly she caught his hand. It took forever before her lashes slowly raised. "You have to stop now."

She stepped away from him, her gaze dropping to the bulge in his tight woolen slacks. Her cheeks became pink as she stared at him. "I'll see about breakfast," she said, forgetting he had already cooked it.

She left and he closed the bathroom door, clenching his fists and closing his eyes. He couldn't remember fighting such a battle with himself over a woman, but he was battling now. He didn't want to hurt her! But he wanted her, wanted to possess her more than he could ever remember desiring a woman in his life.

He finished in the bathroom and quickly headed for the kitchen. At the kitchen door he stopped. She was bending over, getting biscuits out of the oven. The robe hid her figure like a blanket, but in his mind he divested her of the robe and recalled the body he had held against his moments earlier.

"How are the pups today?" he asked, crossing the room.

"Frisky. Want one?"

She looked into his eyes, and her heart thudded against her ribs at the smoldering hunger she saw there.

She wasn't accustomed to being looked at the way Kenneth Holloway was looking at her now. His hand settled on her shoulder, sending tingles down her arm with his touch.

"Does the owner come with the pup?" he asked softly.

She wanted to answer, but she couldn't. His fingers tightened on her shoulder and he leaned closer, smoothing her hair away from her face.

"I don't want to hurt you."

"You won't," she whispered.

"Do you trust everyone this way?"

"Not quite. You're special," she said.

He drew a sharp breath and remembered his resolutions and good intentions. He moved away from her without kissing her, amazed at his feeling of loss.

He sat down to a breakfast of orange juice, coffee, and bacon he had fixed earlier, and scrambled eggs and biscuits she had made. But he was more concerned with the problems at hand, more interested in Camilla than food.

After breakfast Camilla showered and dressed in her jeans and red sweater. She fastened her hair behind her head in a bun again, paused to look at herself, and rummaged in the drawer for makeup, putting on faint touches of mascara and blush. She called the veterinarian and learned that she could pick Drifter up on Sunday after twelve.

When she emerged from the bedroom, Ken was standing a few feet back from the wide picture window in the living room, where he could see down the road. He turned around, and his gaze lowered slowly from her eyes to her throat to her sweater, lingering like a touch, and she felt her body throb.

"How nice you look!" he said in a husky voice.

"Thank you," she answered, trying to keep her wits about her, astounded by the volatile chemistry between them. "I need to make a grocery list, and then I'll go."

In less than an hour he stood at the window again, watching her drive down the road. He had put his life in her hands by trusting her, and he was amazed at himself, because he hadn't known her twenty-four hours.

When an hour passed and she hadn't returned, Ken began to get nervous. Another half hour ticked past, and his anxiety increased. Suddenly he wondered if he had been taken in by big hazel eyes, a soft voice, and sensual, fiery kisses.

Half of him warned him to get out of her house

and away before she came back with the police; the other half told him to trust her implicitly, to wait and see what had delayed her.

As more time passed, his nervousness over what he had done escalated; he decided it was insanity to trust someone he knew so little about. Imagining the police surrounding the house, he pulled on his coat, stuffed food into his pockets, and jammed the revolver into the waistband of his trousers. He was headed for the back door when he heard a car motor.

Feeling as if his heart had stopped, he hurried to the door to see who was coming, half expecting the police. If they had quietly surrounded the house, he would barricade himself inside long enough to call a lawyer. He pulled back the curtain and looked at the empty drive, hearing the car coming around the curve.

His breath caught as he realized there was more at stake now than just facing the police and a murder charge. He had placed his life and future in Camilla's control, because in the brief time they had known each other she had become that important to him. He wanted to trust her. Was she coming back or was it the police?

Five

The small red foreign car came into sight, and Ken felt weak with relief. He hurried to the back door, scanning the area for signs of policemen. He stepped back when she turned the key in the lock.

"Ken! I'm ho—" She broke off when she saw him. Hastily closing the door, she put a bag of groceries on the counter. "I'm sorry it took me so long."

"Yeah, I got worried," he said gruffly, his nerves on edge. "How is it out there?"

"Policemen are everywhere."

"Damn," he said bitterly.

"But I thought of something. When I went down the mountain, they stopped me and looked in the car and asked if they could look in my trunk in case there was some way you could have gotten in there. I opened it and let them look. On the way back they waved me on. The same fellow remembered me and called me by name." For a second she touched her cheek, her fingers lightly brushing the scar. "It's easy for people to remember me."

She said it bluntly, not in a self-pitying manner, but it bothered him that she felt self-conscious when she was so lovely. He touched her cheek. "Don't you realize the guy remembered you because you're an attractive woman?"

She smiled as if humoring him. Then she glanced down, and when he heard her quick intake of breath, he remembered the gun in his waistband, the food in his pockets.

"You were leaving," she said quietly.

He tilted her chin up. "Before you condemn me for not having more trust, let me remind you, you were gone a long, long time. When you left, you said you'd be back in half an hour."

Instantly Camilla realized how nervous he might have become, and for a man who never had much trust in others, he had given her a remarkable amount. "I was delayed by the policeman. He seemed to want to talk and talk, and there was another one who talked to me—" Ken's expression changed from guilt to sardonic amusement, because what she said affirmed his reason for the policeman's having remembered her.

"Two guys talking to a sexy, beautiful broad."

She grinned and shrugged, feeling lighthearted and giddy. "Okay, maybe they do like females."

"Yeah, sure, females. How about one stunning brunette?"

"I'm not! *Stunning* fits me like *shy* would fit you."

"Is that so?" he said, bracing his hand on the refrigerator and hemming her in, leaning closer. He smelled fresh, like her soap, his lips were tempting, his eyes sparkling. "I think when you look in the mirror, you're not seeing the same image men see," he said softly, pulling a pin from her hair.

"What are you doing?"

"Getting rid of the Grandma Moses hairdo. This knot of hair doesn't suit you. I like you much better with your hair down," he added in his deepest voice, and her heart skipped beats.

"Oh, and I've found the pups a home. The policemen are taking them. One is taking two pups and the other is taking one."

"Sight unseen?"

"I gave them a good sales pitch," she answered lightly.

"Oh, yeah. All I'll bet they wanted your phone number so they can call and ask you how to take care of the pups."

Smiling, she looked down, trying to hide the blush that heated her cheeks. "They did want my phone number, but that wasn't why."

"Are they taking the pups home to their little kids? Or did those guys happen to mention they're single?"

She laughed. "They're single. They wanted my phone number, and I said I'd be glad to tell them how to take care of the puppies. That's all they were interested in."

"Sure, sure!" he said, pulling more pins out of her hair.

"That's all I was interested in."

He paused again and an inviting look came into his eyes. But she was aware of the passing of time, and she felt his danger would increase if they waited.

"I've thought about what we can do," she said, trying to sound brisk, sure all he could hear was her pounding heart. "If you get in the trunk of my car, I know they won't want to look in it again. They told me they were doing it for my protection," she said, more aware of his lips, which were enticingly near. She wanted to trail her fingers down the open **V** of his shirt. "We ought to go while the same guys are down there on duty."

"You're right. Did you see any lawmen close to the house who would see us come or go?"

"No, but I pulled into the garage. You're carrying the gun rather conspicuously," she said, yielding to the temptation to touch him. Each brush of his fingers at the back of her head sent dancing tingles in its wake, and it was difficult to concentrate on plans.

"I can't leave the gun here, and I don't have a holster. Any suggestions?"

She shrugged. "No. Once we get past the police, I'll have to find a place where there is the least likely chance of anyone seeing you get out of the trunk, and then you can drive the rest of the way to your condo."

"I have the feeling you already have a place in mind."

"There's a high school parking lot where we'll be out of sight of the street, and no one's in the school because of the Christmas holidays."

"How far to the school?"

"It's about a mile outside of Strawberry Mountain."

"That's good."

"Are you ready to go now?"

When he nodded, she said, "I'll get the puppies."

"I'll get them." His fingers closed on her arms and he stopped her.

"Camilla, this isn't good-bye."

"I know," she said quietly. She forced a smile, but she knew it was good-bye. She wasn't the type of woman Ken Holloway dated. A few kisses meant nothing to him. He might intend to call again, but he wouldn't, and she didn't care to build up her hopes only to have them dashed to pieces later.

They left the house, moving quickly across the yard. She had told Ken he would be safe with her. Now if something happened, it would be disastrous, because he seemed to have put full trust in her.

He folded his legs into the small trunk and gave her a grin. "Watch the bumps."

"I'll hurry."

"Don't worry. I'm okay in here."

She smiled, closed the lid carefully, and rushed to get behind the wheel. Her gaze swept the snowy landscape down the tree-covered slope from the house. A chilling wave of fear came over her, and she clutched the wheel tightly, praying no one would stop them to check the trunk, that no one saw Ken go from the house to the garage.

The first policeman she spotted was walking along the road with a two-way radio, another one only yards behind him on the other side of the road. She waved and stopped to give them the box with the puppies. Telling them she had an appointment, she tried to keep the conversation short. When one of them left to put the box of pups in a squad car, the other one asked her out, and she realized Ken could probably hear every word.

She told the policeman she had to work at the mission and thanked him. As she drove away the two men waved. Returning their wave, she drove ahead out of their sight, winding down the mountain road.

She worried about how Ken was faring in the trunk, but her mind was really on what Ken had said in her kitchen. *Stunning!* He might be one of those men who handed out lavish compliments like greetings, Camilla told herself. It had still sounded wonderful coming from him. She glanced at herself in the mirror. She was attractive, but no one would call her stunning except out of a misguided sense of gratitude or to cajole her into doing something. No matter what arguments her common sense presented, all she could think about was his deep voice telling her she looked stunning.

She signaled and turned, moving into a lane of fast traffic. Soon after she pulled into the high school parking lot. She slowed behind a large Dumpster to park near the rear wing of the snow-covered red-brick building. She hurried to the trunk and unlocked it.

"Are you all right?" she asked Ken.

"Yes. Let's get out of here," he said, climbing out. He slammed the lid and rushed to the driver's seat while she hurried to get in beside him.

He drove swiftly, leaning back and looking relaxed while he watched the road. "Good going. Thanks a million."

"You're welcome."

"And I could tell how overwhelmed they were with the *pups*! Damn, he was coming on to you like a six-wheeler going downhill!"

She laughed and shrugged. "How much farther to your condo?"

"Four miles. I've had this condo for two years now. It's a retreat where I can get off by myself."

"Do you need to do that?"

"Yes. I have to get away from the phone and people who want things from me. It's necessary."

Four miles and he would be gone. Camilla refused to think about it. "What will you do then?"

"I'm going to call one of my lawyers and ask a few questions. I'm going to hire a private investigator. What will you do today?"

Miss you. "I have a shift at the mission late this afternoon and tomorrow afternoon. Other than that—nothing in particular."

"Have you ever been away from your family on Christmas before?"

"No, but I'm needed more here than with them. We'll have a reunion in March and we'll all be together then. We visit each other often. What about your family?"

"About the same as yours," he said, grinning at her. "Our reunion is in the summer. My half brothers and sisters are all younger than I am. Two of them, Glen and Kate, are married."

"Will you have to spend Christmas alone?"

Suddenly his happy expression vanished, and she wished she hadn't asked him.

"I don't plan to stay in hiding too long. I just want to set the wheels in motion on my side. I'll give myself up soon." He shook his head and frowned. "Damn, I don't want to spend Christmas in jail."

"Where had you planned to spend it?"

He glanced at her, and suddenly she realized how much she was prying. Her feminine intuition told her that he had planned to spend Christmas with a woman.

"I'm sorry. It's none of my business."

"Forget it. I was going to spend it in Switzerland skiing with a friend."

Conflict warred within her. There was a woman in his life who was important enough to him to spend Christmas with, and Camilla knew she should keep quiet. On the other hand it seemed most likely he would now be spending Christmas alone at his condo.

She glanced at him, and their gazes met as he took his attention from the road briefly. "What's worrying you?"

"How can you tell I'm worried?"

"I don't know. I can just tell." His voice changed. She detected a note of speculation and wonder in it. "There's some kind of invisible bond between us; each of us responds to the other," he added quietly, and his words were unforgettable.

"We haven't known each other long enough or well enough," she whispered.

"Am I right?"

"Yes," she answered, feeling caught by a force beyond her understanding or control. There *was* an invisible bond between them, as well as a fiery, electric attraction.

"Why are you worried?" he repeated gently.

"I don't want you to spend Christmas alone at your condo."

"I'll be all right." He reached across the seat to give her hand a squeeze, then his attention returned to the road.

She began to believe his theory about a bond, because she knew without asking when they were approaching his condo. They were still on an expressway, and there wasn't any indication in his features that they were near his place, but she knew they were close. He sat back, driving with ease, looking as nonchalant as before.

"We're getting close to your place, aren't we? And it's making you nervous."

He gave her a mocking smile as if to confirm her thoughts, and he nodded. In another few minutes he exited the expressway. They were obviously in a wealthy area. Homes were nestled far back in the pines; the few close to the road were sprawling two-story houses with landscaped yards and winding drives. They neared rock-and-wood town houses that were visible only above the high stone wall surrounding them. Before they reached the turn to the entrance, he began to swear steadily. She was about to ask why, and then she saw the reason.

Six

A police car was approaching from the other direction, its signal blinked as it slowed to turn into the entrance to the town houses.

Ken drove straight past the entrance without slowing, and now she could see the anger in his frown.

"The only person who knows about the condo is my mom," he said, grinding out the words.

"Your mother?" Camilla said, horrified that he might not be able to trust his mother.

"She wouldn't tell the police about it on purpose," he said quickly, to Camilla's relief. "Someone she trusts has tricked her into telling it or wheedled it out of her. It has to be someone closely involved with Walter or with me for her to have given out the information."

"You don't know if that policeman was going to your condo."

She received a sardonic, angry look from him.

"What are the odds that he was there for any other reason?"

They rode through the neighborhood in tense silence. She knew he was mulling over the change in his plans. "I'm trying to think where I can go now. They're probably watching the airport and the bus station."

"You can go home with me," she said quietly. "Let's go back to the high school, and you can get into the trunk again."

"No. I don't want to cause you any trouble."

"Here comes a police car."

"Tell me a joke," Ken said, grinning at her.

"I don't ever remember jokes," she said, looking at him and smiling while her gaze flicked to the police car. Ken was grinning, and she was smiling. She hoped the two policemen wouldn't pay any attention to them because they wouldn't expect Ken to be driving around the city with a woman.

"They're headed in the direction of the condo. Two police cars in this quiet, residential neighborhood seems unlikely. Drive back to the high school, and let's go to my place and think about what you'll do next."

"I hate to have to return to that area. It has as many lawmen as trees."

"It's the only choice you have."

He gave her a rueful grin and turned the car onto the expressway. Back at the high school, he cut the motor. "Are you sure you want to do this?"

She looked into his deep blue eyes and answered honestly. "Absolutely."

He kissed her cheek lightly and climbed out.

She hurried, locking him in the trunk. She drove home without a hitch, talking to a new policeman only briefly when she slowed at the roadblock.

She parked as close to the door as possible, let Ken out of the car, and locked the kitchen door behind them.

As she hung up her parka he swore.

"Someone told Mom a story that made her tell about the condo. I've been thinking about it." He jammed his hands into his pockets. As disheveled and distraught and angry as he was, he was still blatantly handsome, Camilla noted, and her heart was humming along like the car motor over having him with her again.

"Why don't you call the lawyer you had planned to call from the condo, hire an investigator, make whatever calls you need to, and I'll fix lunch?"

He stopped pacing the room, and his expression changed, causing another wild flurry in her pulse as she looked into his eyes. He crossed the room to her, tilting her chin up.

"Thanks, Camilla. Am I glad I like chewing gum," he said, placing his hands on either side of her, leaning close.

"Chewing gum?"

"I wouldn't have dropped my billfold Friday night," he said, but she barely heard the words. His voice enveloped her in its furry warmth.

"You're always hemming me in," she said breathlessly. She trembled as she fought the urge to wrap her arms around his neck. The room heated to tropic steaminess, and her lips parted, because the message in his eyes was unmistakable.

"You don't like being hemmed in?"

"I don't know how to cope with you," she answered honestly.

"I'd say you're coping amazingly well," he whispered. He leaned down to brush her lips with his, to seek and taste, to kiss her passionately, his tongue thrusting over hers in a hungry demand. He crushed her against him, his hand sliding over her contours, exploring each curve down to her thighs.

Camilla was aflame, burning with longing that seemed to have been bottled up all these years, but was uncapped now for Ken. She twisted against his strong frame, moaning softly, unconcerned with her response, swept up in his kisses, from which reason had flown on giddy wings.

Finally she leaned back and wiggled out of his arms. He released her instantly, but he had a dazed expression in his eyes that made her want to raise her lips to his for another kiss.

"Maybe you'd better make those phone calls," she said quietly.

"Yeah, sure." He lifted a long strand of her soft brown hair and ran it across his cheek. "You're beautiful, Camilla."

"Thank you," she answered, sounding dubious, touching her cheek lightly. He caught her hand, his brows drawing together in a frown.

"You're conscious of scars; I'm conscious of a very passionate, warm, beautiful woman."

His words were spoken slowly, distinctly, and with all the conviction possible. She felt tears sting her eyes, and she threw her arms around his neck, clinging to him tightly. "You're special, Kenneth Holloway," she whispered in his ear as his arms wrapped around her. "Just be honest with me. I'm a real sucker where people are concerned," she tried to add lightly, but it came out in a shaky voice. She didn't want him to know how deeply his words had affected her, that she was crying over them, or that she felt absolutely vulnerable with him.

"I know you're a sucker where people are concerned," he said gently, stroking her back. "Anyone who's sappy enough to turn down a monetary reward for returning a wallet is a sucker."

Gaining control of her emotions, she laughed.

Deep in her heart she felt he was the one love of her life. And she was firmly convinced that he would not truly love her in return. For years now she had not expected anything from others. If they gave her their friendship or love, she took it as a special gift, and it always came as a marvelous surprise.

She had known Ken so briefly, yet time had nothing to do with her feelings for him. Absolutely nothing. Time couldn't create that electric tension that sprang to life between them so easily. Nor could it give each of them an insight into the other's thoughts and emotions.

Her cheek was pressed to his soft, woolen coat. She pulled away to look at him, and his eyes were filled with concern that changed swiftly to desire. "I can't look at you without wanting you."

She wanted him to desire her, to kiss her until she melted. He groaned as he watched her, and she suspected her thoughts were as discernible to him as if she had spoken them aloud. He pulled her back roughly, kissing her hard, making her blood thunder in her veins before she finally broke away.

"You can use the phone in the bedroom. It'll be quieter."

"You won't bother me if I don't bother you," he said, pulling off his coat and reaching for a phone book. "I've hired one of these guys before for business, a routine job, and he was good. If only I can recognize the name. I have it on file in my office, but a lot of good that does now."

"Would you like grilled cheese sandwiches for lunch?"

"Sure, that's great," he said, but his mind was on the names in the phone book. "Jesse Early. He's the fellow I hired."

While she worked quietly he talked to the investigator, making arrangements, telling him what he wanted, avoiding giving any indication of where he was. Next he called an attorney named John, and again told all that he had told Camilla earlier. As she listened to it for the third time an idea came to her. She placed a bowl of crisp golden potato chips on the table and poured two mugs of steaming black coffee, handing one to Ken while he talked. She watched him run his fingers through his hair. His brow was creased in a frown; his shirt pulled tautly across his shoulders. He sounded cool and collected, but Camilla knew how worried he was. After he replaced the receiver, he looked at her. "Damn, I just don't know *why*. I didn't know anyone hated me like that."

"You said there's enough money involved to make someone your enemy."

"There is. But it gives me a funny feeling. And

my anger at Walter and his devious and ruthless ways—it's finally gone. I don't think I'll ever view life the same as I did before this weekend," he said solemnly.

"I waited to put the cheese sandwiches in until you were ready so they will be hot."

"Wait just a few more minutes," he said, standing up. "I have two more calls to make."

He left the room, and she knew he was going to call a woman. Or women. He wanted privacy. She watched him stride out of the room, and her heart seemed to go with him. The room was empty and silent without him, and she wondered if talking to another woman would change the way he felt toward her. When he returned, he walked into the room, straight to her, and slipped his arms around her, taking a plate from her hand and setting it on the table.

"It's been at least a quarter of an hour since I held you in my arms. Too long."

"It has been, at that," she said, wrapping her arms around his narrow waist, reassured by his actions. He kissed her, and after a moment she said, "Your lunch is getting cold. Come on."

He smiled at her and sat down.

"At three I have to go to the mission to work."

"Oh, Lordy," he said, frowning. "I'll be shut up here alone with nothing to do."

"Is that so terrible?" she asked with amusement.

"Yes!" he snapped, and her amusement vanished instantly. In spite of his calm exterior she knew his nerves were raw from having to trust others to work out his problem.

"Hell, I don't have any appetite. It's not your cooking." He put down his sandwich.

"Maybe I should do something to make you forget your worries for a moment," she said in what she hoped was a sultry voice as she pressed her foot against his.

As swiftly as his anger had surfaced, it was gone. He focused on her, smiled, and she could see the stiffness leave his shoulders.

"Keep that up and you might succeed."

As soon as his plate was empty, after he had refilled their cups with coffee, she said, "I've been thinking about what you told me. And I heard you go over it again when you made your phone calls. Go back and tell me one more time what Walter Poplin said to you before he died."

"I think he said, 'Knew you would be here.' I don't know if he meant the murderer or me."

"Go on with the rest of it."

"'. . . framed . . . set up because the money . . . knew everything . . . it was more than . . . wanted all. . . .' "

He waited while she thought it over. "You know, you said it didn't all make sense and some words were slurred?"

He nodded. "What's on your mind?"

"I've been thinking about the four men you named. Suppose Walter didn't say, 'It was more than . . . wanted all.' "

"Oh, Lordy," Ken snapped, instantly guessing what she was about to suggest. "He could have been saying it was Moreland . . . or maybe Garland, but Moreland fits. 'It was Moreland—he wanted all,' may have been what Walter said. Moreland!"

She nodded, seeing the shock in his expression. He ran his hand across the back of his neck. "That may be it! I'm going to call Jesse Early." Suddenly he leaned forward, grabbing her shoulders tightly. "Aren't you the smart one!" He kissed her quickly, and then he stretched his arm out, tilting his chair back to reach for the phone. He talked briefly with the investigator while Camilla cleared the table. When he hung up the phone, he pushed back his chair with a scrape, caught her as she reached for the coffeepot and swung her down onto his lap.

"What a brain!"

"Logical deduction, good guess, luck maybe."

"Let me show you my thanks," he said playfully, and they were lost to passionate kisses that drove all worries away.

"I hate to stop this," she whispered, kissing his throat, winding her fingers in his thick hair, "but I have something else that has to be done." She scooted off his lap. "How are you with a needle and thread?"

"Terrible. With my sisters and my mom around, I didn't have to sew and I haven't had to since I left home either. Are you missing a button?" he asked, running his hand down her neck.

She laughed and wiggled out of reach. "No. Come watch while I sew. If I knew you were coming, I'd have done this sooner. I thought I'd have time on my hands, and I took some clothes for the mission from a friend of mine, but some items need mending. I want to take them to the mission when I go today."

He lifted the box from the corner of the kitchen and carried it to the living room. She curled up near the fire to sew while he paced the room and drank coffee. After half an hour she knew his nerves were about stretched to their limit.

"You're too accustomed to being in charge," she said, threading the needle again.

"Yes, I am. I hate this."

He clenched his fists, and suddenly she realized how difficult it would be for him if he turned himself in to the police and had to stay in a cell. She closed her eyes, praying the murderer would be found soon.

"Camilla?" he asked quietly. When she opened her eyes, he said, "I thought you might have fallen asleep."

"No, I was thinking. You won't like staying here while I'm at work."

"You have an alternative?"

"Yes, I do. Come with me to the mission."

"That's crazy."

"No, it's not," she said calmly. "The police would never look for you at the Sunshine Mission; not for Mr. Kenneth Holloway of Holloway Enterprises. The people there are nice, very nice. We don't have security officers, and no one would expect you to be in that place."

"No, but thanks," he said with a smile.

"You'd rather stay here alone and pace the floor? You may wear out my carpet."

He made another turn around the room and

stopped by the fire. "What about the mission people?" he asked, and she knew he wanted to go.

"They don't ask questions. And there's a kind of loyalty down there. People down on their luck stick together."

"Lady, you do trust people!" he snapped with a snort of disgust. "I'll stay here."

"Suit yourself, my friend. I'm going to comb my hair and then I have to go."

She went to her room and started to put her hair in the usual bun, then remembered what he had said. She plaited it and let it hang down her back, wondering if he would like the braid any better than he had liked the bun. The house was silent, she found him at the window, staring outside.

"Ken, I'm leaving."

"Look, if I go down there, I'll have to wear something different. What I have on is too obvious."

She glanced at the slacks to his suit, which were probably custom-made and expensive. "I know." She dug through the box of discarded clothing and came up with a pair of men's jeans and a sweater. "These are clean. Want to wear them?"

"The jeans and sweater will be fine. Give me two minutes," he said, snatching the clothes out of her hand.

He returned in less than that time, and she paused to look at him, laughter bubbling up inside her.

"My, oh my, are you the handsome devil! Whooie, do those jeans fit!"

He grinned. "I don't think I can sit down, but they fit."

"If you just weren't so dad-burned handsome," she drawled, and he grabbed her around the waist.

"Do tell me more!" he said with just as much of a drawl.

"I think we better go!"

"Coward. Very well, back into the trunk of the car. And pray the jeans don't split."

"Oh, we can't use your real name. What shall I call you?"

"I don't care. You pick something."

"Now who's trusting?"

"Where you're concerned—I don't have a qualm," he said as one of his unpredictable changes occurred, and he switched from lighthearted banter to earnest words. "Another thing. Can you stop at a store and get some things for me? I'll repay you for everything."

"You don't need to repay me."

With a disarming smile he continued, "Will you pick up a bottle of white wine, either Californian or Spanish? And will you stop at any clothing store and get me a few things? I'll give you a list of my sizes. If I eat dinner, I won't be able to wear these jeans tomorrow."

She laughed, and together they sat down to make a list.

Finally they rushed to the car. Camilla felt vulnerable because it would be so easy to be seen if someone were prowling around the area.

"Into the trunk with you," she said, after he'd deposited the box of clothes on the back seat. "Is it terrible in there?"

"It's better than jail," he answered grimly. "Let's go, love." The word rolled easily off his tongue, surprising him, because he wasn't casual with endearments, and he wasn't a man who used them often. Camilla didn't seem to notice, but he knew she had. And he knew she would think he used the word lightly. She gave him one last look, and he realized how much she hated closing him into the narrow space. When he saw her concern for him, something seemed to tighten inside his chest. His need for her was building with startling momentum. She didn't expect to date him later, but he intended that they would, even if he had to fight a battle with her. Then she was gone, and he was enveloped in darkness.

They drove to the high school, where he climbed out of the trunk and rode in the front seat with her. She stopped twice to make purchases for him, carrying the packages back to the car.

Ken drove to the mission, located in the old part of the city on the fringe of downtown, an area now full of empty apartments. A garage and body shop was across the street on the corner; a two-story abandoned house on another corner. The Sunshine Mission was a stucco building with cracked windows and peeling paint. It was bordered by a narrow sidewalk, and a hand-lettered cardboard sign with the mission's name was propped in the front window.

They parked in back. Ken climbed out and carried the big box of clothing along a shoveled path to the back door.

Inside the aromas of stew and coffee were inviting. A fresh coat of pale green paint had renewed the walls in the dining room, but the rest of the place needed work. Serving lines were formed at a waist-high partition dividing the kitchen and the dining room. As they walked through the room Ken realized how out of touch with the world he had become.

Occupied with his businesses, chasing after fun with as much zest as he did money, he realized he had forgotten how bad life could sometimes become. And then he focused his attention on Camilla. She was like a bright bouquet of flowers on a cold winter's day, bringing a smile to everyone who saw her.

"Jerry, this is my friend—" There was only a moment's hesitation before she said, "Duke. Duke, meet Jerry."

Ken shook hands, grinning at her selection of a name.

"Glad to meet you," Jerry said. "Any friend of Millie's is a friend of mine."

"Think it'll snow?" she asked him, and Jerry laughed.

"I'll keep watching for a flake to fall, kid."

"You do that, Jerry." They kept on walking into a crowded room, and he saw immediately that Camilla had been correct when she had said he would be safe there. The police wouldn't look for him in the group of homeless people.

When he had a chance, he leaned close. "Duke?"

"It fits you," she said dryly. "We all go by first names. If you need a last name, I think Frisco would be a good one."

"Duke Frisco. I knew I could trust you."

Her smile was constant as she introduced him

to some of the people who stayed there and some who worked there. In a quiet way with just a remark or two, she always brought smiles to the others' faces.

Within an hour he had met too many people to remember, and he had been handed an apron and knife and given a job peeling potatoes.

He worked diligently at a task he hadn't done since he was a kid, watching Camilla when he could, reassessing his life as the pile of peelings grew.

In less than twenty-four hours he had been through trauma and violent changes. And he had met Camilla. She was special to him, and she was growing more and more so every minute.

A man shuffled to the door of the kitchen. His suit was threadbare and he needed a shave. He gave everyone a wave and a toothless grin. Camilla raised her voice to such a level, Ken decided the man must be a little deaf.

"Hi, Charley!"

" 'Lo, pretty lady."

"Go on, you say that to all the ladies!"

He chuckled and moved on to talk to others in the dining room, but in that moment, Ken realized that when Camilla was at work here, she lost her self-consciousness. In spite of the people and the time and the place, he wanted to touch her.

Instead, he peeled faster, wondering if all the potatoes in Colorado had been donated to the mission.

It was eleven when they stepped out the back door to go home. Snow drifted down, big wet flakes swirling and falling on Camilla's cheeks. "Ready for a trunk ride?"

"Yeah. I may fall asleep on this ride."

"Little hard work back there in the kitchen?"

"Do you work like that every time you come?"

"Summer isn't so busy. But with snow and bad weather, more people have to get off the streets and find shelter."

"You're a pretty good kid," he said lightly, giving her shoulders a squeeze and leaving his arm around her.

"You're not so bad yourself, old-timer."

The roadblocks were gone when she drove home, and she told Ken as soon as he stepped out of the car.

"With the roadblocks gone, I don't see why you'd have to ride—"

Her words were snapped off as his hand closed on her arm.

Ken spun her around, his arms banding around her like steel, crushing her to him. "I've been waiting for this for hours."

Her heart thudded and seemed to stop as she looked up at him. Snowflakes turned to crystal drops on his lashes and the look he gave her was enough to melt every flake in the yard. She slipped her arms around his neck and stood on tiptoe. "Hi, Duke."

"Hi, Very Special Person."

"Who, me?"

"Positively you," he replied, smiling at her. "I think I've been swept off my feet," he said, and she wondered if he was teasing.

"Speaking of feet—mine are freezing. We're getting snowed on, and it's warm in the house."

"Do you really care?"

"I keep wondering when you'll stop talking and kiss—"

His smile vanished, and his mouth met hers in a slow, searing kiss that made her forget the cold.

"Let's go inside," he whispered in her ear. "If you don't mind, I'm changing into my new duds. These don't fit."

"The new ones might not either."

"They will," he said cheerfully. "And I'm going to make a phone call to Jesse Early and see if anything has developed," he said over his shoulder as they entered the house.

Humming a tune, she made hot chocolate and carried it into the living room, where he had already built a fire. Flames danced in the fireplace; the logs, crackling and popping. The police were gone from the area, and the only light in the room was the fire, so she pulled the drapes open on the wide picture window behind the Christmas tree. Light snow was falling, flakes drifting silently to the ground. She sat down on the floor near the fire to wait for Ken.

In minutes he reappeared in crisp new jeans and a gray sweater. His hair was combed back in smooth waves, but with the dampness in the air two recalcitrant locks were already beginning to curl over his wide forehead. His frown told her as much as his words.

"You have bad news from the detective."

"Yes. Garland Vickers is in the hospital with a slipped disk. Alan Moreland is in Arizona for the weekend; he's due back tomorrow. John Edwards had a Christmas party last night, and his time is accounted for all evening. Bob Jensen was with one of my men all evening, talking about the company and the changes I intend to make."

"So I was probably wrong."

"I think you were right," he said, sitting on the floor beside her, his right side to the fire. He was silent, lost in thought while they sipped the hot chocolate.

"I asked Jesse to see if he could get any leads on a hired killer."

"You think someone paid another person to commit the crime?" she asked in surprise.

"It was carefully planned, and so far all of the men have airtight alibis. Moreland was at a convention Friday night and seen by dozens of people. No way could he have gotten back here and then returned to Arizona. Same with Garland. But I think you're right. Walter said Moreland, and I thought he was saying 'More than.' "

"You know, if you'd like, there are some people at the mission who I would trust to ask about a hired killer and keep quiet about the reason."

"Those people don't look like the type to associate with a hired killer."

"There are all types of people at the mission, some down on their luck temporarily—families passing through town who run out of funds and get caught in a storm—and there are people who come in regularly who are streetwise. They have a lot of contacts."

"Sure, go ahead and ask. If and when I ever get back to my own home, I'll be happy to pay someone a very tidy sum for information." He ran his fingers through his hair and looked at her solemnly. "I've been giving a lot of thought to what I should do if something doesn't break on this case."

Her heart began to drum, and she waited expectantly, barely daring to hope that he would be with her a little longer.

"If it weren't for Christmas, I'd wait one more day and then I would turn myself in, but the thought of spending Christmas locked up—you said you were staying in town to work at the mission. Do—"

She interrupted him quickly. "Stay with me."

"You're sure?" he asked, and she smiled. He would be with her for Christmas!

She nodded, and he winked at her. "Thanks. If that's the case, I'll get you to drop me off some place far, far from here on Saturday, the day after Christmas, and I'll turn myself in to the police." He placed his empty cup on the hearth. "I can't do anything else about the problem tonight, so I want to forget about it now. I called Mom and told her I'm all right." He locked his fingers behind his head, the gold watch gleaming in the firelight.

"I asked about the condo. She said a man called and told her he was Ben Wertly, my V.P., and he desperately needed to get in touch with me because an emergency had come up in Dallas, et cetera, et cetera. He kept on until she gave him the address and phone number of the condo. Ben Wertly is a fictitious name."

"How did someone know to call her and ask?"

"A select few knew that I go somewhere to get away, and that in a real crisis they can call her.

Walter knew it, and who knows whom he told! At any rate the detective and my lawyer and Mom don't know where I am, so I'm safe for the time being. Now, let's get on to more interesting things." As he talked his voice softened and changed, dropping a notch, and his gaze locked with hers while he began to unfasten her long plait of hair. She felt the gentle tugs on her scalp, his fingers brushing against her back; every touch sent sparks dancing along her veins.

Finally her hair fell free over her shoulders, and he lifted it away to kiss the nape of her neck. Sparks changed to molten heat. With a groan he pulled her into his arms, cradling her head against his shoulder while he leaned over her to kiss her, and Camilla was lost in a whirlwind of passion.

They spent the next few hours in front of the fire in each other's arms. Ken's kisses forged chains around her heart that she knew could never be completely broken. At moments she saw how tense he was, and she knew each passing hour increased his worries because he didn't seem any closer to a solution and he didn't like being a fugitive.

Saturday night she talked to three men at the mission—Barney, Murph, and Joel—who promised to help.

The next day was Sunday. The sun was shining, giving a blue tint to the sparkling snow. The air was crisp and clear and invigorating when she stepped outside to get the paper.

Dread filled her at the thought of Ken reading about himself, but she knew he was waiting. Finished with breakfast, he sat at the table wearing a pale blue sweatshirt and jeans.

Church was out of the question, Camilla told herself. Early that morning she had pulled on jeans and a yellow sweater, and her hair was brushed to a high sheen, falling loosely over her shoulders.

Ken pulled a chair close to his and watched her unfold the paper. "Here it comes," he said, bracing for the news.

"Don't look at it," she said. "It won't help you any."

"I'm too curious, and I want to know what the police say."

"I can read it and tell you," she said, wishing he would let her, because she knew the articles would upset him.

He took the paper and shook it out. The same smiling picture of him the policemen had shown to her was on the front page, and the headline seemed to scream the news in black letters: EXECUTIVE'S SON SOUGHT IN FATAL SHOOTING.

He unfolded the bottom half of the paper, and her gaze jumped to the lower part of the page. A beautiful blonde, whose face was familiar to Camilla, was smiling at the camera. It was easy to read the bold print. **Model Has No Knowledge of Suspect's Whereabouts.**

Camilla felt an icy chill as she stared at the picture. Reality intruded now, bursting the bubble of intimacy she'd shared with Ken during the past two days. As she studied the picture she knew she had seen the same face on many magazine covers. It was Sheryl Anderson, a model who did cosmetic, clothing, and car ads. She was truly stunning.

He swore angrily as he read the lead article, oblivious of the woman's picture at the bottom of the page or Camilla's reaction to it. She scanned the words swiftly: *. . . spend holidays in Switzerland. She has had no contact with Holloway. "He is innocent; Ken would never commit such a crime. I know him so well; under no circumstances would he do this. . . ."*

Camilla stared at the picture again. Sheryl Anderson. Beautiful, successful, sophisticated Sheryl Anderson. She was the perfect type for Ken.

Camilla had known all along that they were from two different worlds, but for the past few hours she was beginning to shut the future out so firmly that she had forgotten about it. She picked up some dishes and carried them to the sink.

In a moment he swore again, one word said under his breath. She heard the paper rattle and the scrape of his chair and then he was turning her to face him.

"Sheryl and I are good friends, but it's not a serious involvement. And that was before I met you," he said.

"Ken, you don't have to explain. We don't have any ties to each other—and we never will. I know that. I've always known it."

"How can you say that to me after everything we've shared?" he asked. He sounded angry, more disturbed than she could have imagined possible.

"Because I'm realistic."

"Haven't I given you every indication of wanting to continue seeing you when this is over?"

"I know you say that, but who knows how you'll feel in the future?"

"For someone who can be so damn trusting, you picked a lousy time to stop!" he snapped.

"I trust you. I believe you. Tomorrow doesn't exist. I don't like to build dreams and wild expectations. If I don't expect anything, then I won't be disappointed."

Her words cut into him like a knife. She was too sweet, too lovely, and too good to people simply to give without hoping for something in return.

"Camilla, you see the cloudy sky while I know there's a sun still shining behind the clouds. Dammit, expect more of people!"

"Sometimes trust and expectation are two different things," she said quietly.

"Why am I getting all worked up over this?" he asked, his voice at a near shout. He paused, then said softly, "I guess I'll just have to prove to you how I feel."

He pulled her to him, ignoring her feeble protest about wet hands and running water. He kissed her until she was clinging to him and he was satisfied that he had driven the demons that had been stirred by the picture of Sheryl away.

When he released Camilla, he reached behind her to turn off the faucet. "You were right, I shouldn't have read the news."

"It'll be time to go to the mission soon, and

you'll be able to forget your troubles there. And I can bring Drifter home before we go to the mission. I'll go get him and introduce you to him. Just give him time. Drifter is a watchdog, after all. And he's very loyal to me."

"Smart pooch."

She winked at him and went back to rinsing dishes. Her cheerful attitude made him feel better.

At one o'clock she picked up Drifter and brought him home, letting him bound out of the car into the fenced backyard that ran up the mountainside. When she entered the house, Ken kissed her in greeting, and then together they went outside.

"Drifter, down, boy," she said. "He'll make friends with you soon since you're with me."

The shaggy dog barked once, and Ken knelt down, his arm propped on his thigh, his hand hanging down while he talked quietly to the dog. In seconds Drifter was happily pawing Ken's hand and wagging his tail.

"My, you do have a way with dogs and women!" she exclaimed. "Look at him wag his tail."

Ken stood up, holding her shoulders. "Let's see what I have to do to get you to do the same."

Laughing, she gave him a hard shove and caught him off guard. He tumbled backward and would have been all right, only he sidestepped to avoid Drifter, who was beginning to enjoy their fun. Ken fell into a snowbank, and Camilla yelped, running for the door. She almost had it closed behind her when Ken burst inside and caught her, pulling her into his arms. "I ought to drag you back outside and throw you down in the snow," he said in mock anger as he watched her.

Snowflakes fell from his hair, grazing her cheek as they tumbled down. "Instead, I think I'll settle for kissing you until you faint."

"Grand choice! Absolutely the right one," she murmured as she put her arms around him, oblivious of the snow.

Other news moved Walter's murder off the front page of the paper; Christmas was getting closer, and Camilla finally faced the fact that she was head over heels in love. She knew she would get hurt. She didn't belong in Ken's world, and he had never told her he loved her. She had no illusions as to what would happen when the murderer was found and Ken was cleared.

Yet she loved him. He was her first true love, and deep in her heart she felt she would love him all the rest of her life. And while each day brought them closer to Christmas and to parting, she closed her mind to the future. She intended to live only in the present; tomorrow didn't exist.

Seven

They fell into a routine that would never become dull to Camilla. Ken went to the mission each day with her. On Monday he changed the system for distributing clothing, making the method more efficient, and to her delight as the days passed, he became friends with everyone he met.

Wednesday night while Ken was cooking a huge vat of spaghetti, Joel came in the door and called him aside. Camilla was busy setting the table, but she glanced over her shoulder once and noticed Joel and Ken in conversation. The next time she looked they had disappeared down the hall.

No longer worrying about being seen, Ken drove home that night. He was unusually quiet, and they rode in silence.

"Joel gave me a name to check on tonight," he said finally. "I'll get in touch with Jesse as soon as we get to your house."

He was so quiet on most of the drive that she

knew he was tense, worried over time and the lack of developments.

"I won't be long," Ken said, flinging off his coat then picking up the phone to call. Camilla pulled off her red parka, hung it in the closet, and went to the bedroom to brush her hair. The image she saw in the mirror bore little resemblance to the way she had looked such a short time ago.

She wore her hair loose the way Ken liked it. Above her yellow sweater and faded jeans her cheeks were pink from the cold, and she wore light touches of makeup. She looked different, but it wasn't altogether because of her hair or makeup. There was an inner glow that hadn't been evident before, and it was because of Kenneth Holloway. She leaned closer, studying her face, touching a scar on one cheek. She didn't think about the scars as much because Ken didn't seem to notice them or care, and she would never understand why he didn't, because he was so incredibly handsome. She went back to the kitchen, wanting to be with him as much as possible.

He sat by the phone, rubbing the back of his neck.

"Did you talk to Jesse?" she asked, quickly getting a pot of coffee brewing.

"Yeah, I talked with both of them, Jesse and John. They'll work on it. You know, you're as bad a coffee addict as I am."

"My only vice," she said merrily, realizing she was able to answer Ken with a casual lightness in her tone that she had never been able to achieve around a man before.

"Is that so?" he asked with a flicker of a smile, but then he was lost in silence, staring into space.

By this time she had learned enough about him to know that when he became tense with worry, activity was the best solution. Before Friday night she was sure he had channeled his energies constantly into work or play, and suddenly to be unable to do either was too confining for him.

"How about building a snowman?"

"You're kidding! After the dishes I washed tonight! And it's midnight. People don't build snowmen in the dead of night."

"Excuses, excuses! If there's a snowman in the front yard, *Duke*, do you think the police will suspect you're living here and built it?"

He grinned and threw up his hands. "What would I do without you?"

"Starve, hide in the woods, be bored to pieces." She tossed him an inexpensive brown parka he'd asked her to buy, and she pulled on her red jacket and gloves.

While Drifter played in the yard they worked hard rolling up a big ball of snow and then adding to it.

"Let's make it a snow dog—"

"Nope," he said. "Just a plain old snowman, or you'll have some newspaper photographer up here to take a picture of your imaginative creation. Nope. Just a snowman." All the time he talked, he was working as if he were getting paid to finish the job within the hour, and she suspected he was letting out some of his frustration.

When they had a body and head with two small clods of dirt for eyes, Camilla couldn't resist. She scooped up a handful of snow, packed it, shaped it into a ball, and let it fly. It smashed against Ken's shoulder, sending sprinkles of snow over his neck.

He yelled, turning instantly to come after her. She shrieked and ran as fast as she could until he tackled her and they both fell.

She screamed as cold snow poured down her collar and over her face. Ken jumped to his feet, picking up a handful of snow.

"No, you don't!" she yelled as she tried to get away. But he caught her. They both fell, rolling together until Ken was on top. He laughed at her while Drifter barked happily at them.

"I'm freezing."

"If you're really freezing, you wouldn't sound so happy."

"I'm happy because you're here."

Neither his expression nor his voice revealed any reaction to her statement. All he said was, "Race you for the house."

"Okay."

He stood up and started to run, but she rolled on her stomach and caught his ankle, yanking him down, so she could sprint for the house. He passed her, raced up the steps and slammed the door, locking her out.

"Ken!" she called, pounding on the door. "Open this door! Kenneth Hollo—"

The door flew open, and he yanked her inside, slamming and locking it again behind her. "Will you shut up and not announce to the world I'm here!" he said, but he was grinning and shedding his coat and boots as quickly as possible. She pulled hers off, too, hopping up and down from the cold.

"Brrr. I can't wait to get in front of the fire. Thank heavens I put the coffee on before we went outside."

She hurried into the living room where a fire was crackling and the scent of pine filled the room along with the smell of brewed coffee.

She glanced over her shoulder at Ken. His cheeks were red from the snow and his hair had curled from the dampness.

She rubbed her hands and held them out to the fire.

They both laughed as they remembered their antics, but then merriment died, and he pulled her into a tight embrace.

"You're good for me. This could have gone a whole different way if I hadn't met you," he said, aware it was a vast understatement. She was a marvel to him, and the more he knew her, the more he wanted to be with her.

She clung to him, knowing he had changed her like a stream that, deluged by rain, cuts a new channel and changes its course. "It'll work out. It has to. They'll find the right man."

"I hope so, but it's only in the movies that it 'has to.' " He framed her face with his hands. "Tomorrow is Christmas Eve. I can't go shopping to get you anything."

"Don't be ridiculous. You don't have to give me a present."

His gaze drifted to her mouth, and her lips parted eagerly, her breath coming out as a sweet sigh . . . and he was overcome with desire for her. She was so fine, intelligent, sensual beyond his wildest dreams—he wanted her with the hunger of a starving man. It took only the faintest touch to evoke an instant response from her. His body reacted intensely to his thoughts, and he tightened his arms around her, leaning over to kiss her as if she were the only woman in the world.

Camilla's heart thudded violently, because Ken's kiss conveyed the depth of his need. She clung to him, her softness pressed to his lean frame, his arousal hard against her in spite of the clothing between them. His hands slipped beneath her bulky yellow sweater and were warm on her flesh, making her moan softly. With a swift movement he tugged the sweater over her head and flung it aside.

For a moment, frankly and without embarrassment, she waved her hand. "I have scars from the wreck."

"I don't give a damn," he said gruffly, seeing only one small scar across her shoulder.

His hands rested on her slender waist while his gaze acted like a flame, a caress, that hardened her nipples and brought tingles to her skin.

"How beautiful you are!"

His voice was a rasp. He made her feel as if she were the most gorgeous woman in the world. She wanted to touch him, to look at him as well. She reached for a button on his shirt and he sucked in his breath as if he had received a blow to his midsection.

"I'm so . . . inexperienced," she said softly, revealing a remnant of the shyness she had shown when he had first met her.

"Oh, Camilla . . ." With a groan he leaned forward to kiss her through her white lacy bra.

Lost in a giddy spiral of sensation, Camilla closed her eyes. His lips grazed her flesh lightly, yet it was a scorching touch. Then he flicked open the catch to her bra, pushing it off her shoulders.

His strong hands cupped her breasts as he lavished honeyed kisses on her, and she trembled with longing. Her hands fumbled with his buttons, finally slipping beneath his shirt to caress and explore his chest in a way she had longed to do since the first night she'd met him.

His thumbs drew circles around the twin peaks of her breasts, which throbbed with desire, while she tugged at his belt, feeling engulfed in a haze of delicious agony.

Ken was burning with need, astounded at the intensity of his response . . . and hers. He would wager all he owned that he was the first man to get close to her. Yet she was totally responsive, more provocative because of her unbridled abandon, and she made him feel like the luckiest man on earth. He fought for control, wanting to take time to pleasure her, but he was hot, ablaze with a hunger he didn't think could ever be assuaged.

He rained kisses on her smooth flesh as if he could forge invisible chains around her heart to bind her to him forever. And he was lost in his love for her, finally acknowledging what he had felt since the first night, whispering to her, "I love you."

Above the drumming of her heartbeat Camilla heard him, and whispered words she meant to last forever in return: "I love you." Then words and thoughts were gone, lost to incredible sensations that ignited every nerve. He peeled away her clothing, holding her away from him to look at her. At the same time her gaze devoured him shamelessly.

As her fingers locked in his hair, he knelt to kiss her heated skin, stroking and touching until she dropped to her knees and flung her arms around him. He pulled her down on the floor, rolling to his side, sliding his leg between hers. Trailing kisses to her ear, he said, "Camilla, I'll take precautions. You'll be protected, love."

"*Love.*" She wanted him to an extent she didn't know she could want a man. "Ken, please," she whispered, aching for him, hurting, feeling incomplete.

He moved over her, pausing a moment to drink in the sight of her while she did the same, memorizing every detail of his virile body; his throbbing manhood, his strong, muscled thighs.

She held out her arms and he came down gently, thrusting slowly into her, his mouth covering hers as she raised her hips to meet him.

"I don't want to hurt you," he whispered. In return her arms tightened around him.

He heard her quick gasp, and he tried to go slowly, tried to hold back because he knew he had hurt her momentarily. But then she began to move in response and he was lost. Control evaporated; all he could feel was a burning, throbbing need for her.

Camilla rocked with sensations that drove her to abandon. She called his name because she couldn't get enough of him and in turn she heard his words of love to her, his harsh groan as his body shuddered with release at the same time ecstasy burst within her, radiating in shock waves that stormed her senses.

They lay entwined, hearts beating in unison. She buried her head in his shoulder, kissing him, loving him.

He kissed her temple, her cheek, her throat, murmuring his love. He raised up to look at her. His blue eyes darkened to indigo as he studied her. They both smiled, satiated with love and pleasure.

He turned on his side to look at her. "Hurt?"

"Of course not. Do I act like I hurt?"

He kissed the corner of her mouth. "You are the most incredible, marvelous, delectable morsel a man ever encountered."

"I'm delectable?"

"Definitely! Delectable, devastating, delicious."

"Did you say delicious or delirious?" she asked, squinting her eyes at him in mock suspicion.

"Maybe it is delirious, but I thought it was delicious. Let me taste and see," he said, leaning forward to kiss her again. To her amazement in minutes she felt his arousal and her own need rise, like flames fanned back to life in a wind.

The night became a dream of passion; moments

that would be indelibly etched in her memory forever, moments that bound her heart and soul as well as her body to Ken.

By dawn they were on the edge of sleep, locked in each other's arms in her bed. She squeezed his shoulder tightly. "Merry Christmas, Ken."

"That's tomorrow," he answered drowsily. "This is Christmas Eve morning."

"And I got my present last night. The very best."

He turned to kiss her. "You're quite a woman." He settled back, and she was content to lie against him with her eyes closed, holding him tightly to her. She couldn't sleep as she thought about them. The night had been cataclysmic, transforming her into a whole woman because he had given her a sense of assurance of her own appeal, something she would never lose and something that she knew would affect the quality of her life deeply. She smiled and sighed, opening her eyes to glance at him.

His lashes were dark on his cheeks, his jaw firm, his muscular chest rising and falling regularly. He had given her so much, he had changed her, and he seemed to have needed her as desperately as she had wanted him. Her eyes fluttered closed.

Later that morning she told him she had to get groceries for Christmas dinner. She already had a turkey out of the freezer and thawing when she left. She made three stops to get groceries and Christmas presents for Ken.

She had given it a lot of thought all week, knowing he probably bought everything he wanted for himself. She had no idea about his tastes or hobbies. She knew so little about the material trappings of his life, yet she knew so much about his emotions and desires. The first two gifts were easy to buy; the last she had to debate over as she stood in her favorite art gallery and looked at a small bronze statue that she loved. It was a beautiful reproduction of an eagle in flight just settling on a limb, its wings still spread wide. It would be a lasting gift. It was special to her, and she wanted it to be special to Ken. Making her decision, she purchased it with her savings and waited while the gift was boxed and wrapped.

She hid the presents in the trunk of the car and arrived home in time for lunch.

After lunch they had two hours before they had to leave for the mission. As they sat in the front room and drank coffee by the fire, he asked her. "What are your Christmas traditions?"

"We open presents Christmas morning, and later we have a big dinner; then everyone over twenty takes a nap. The kids are always too excited to sleep."

"Aunt Camilla."

"No, Aunt Millie. You're the only one who calls me Camilla."

"Do you mind?"

She squeezed his hand. "Don't ever stop," she said softly.

He pulled her hand up and kissed her knuckles, asking between kisses, "Aren't you going to miss being with your family?"

"Not when I'm with you," she said with a candor that he found refreshing. The women he had known paled in comparison to Camilla. He wanted to give her a marvelous present just to see her eyes sparkle. He watched her now, her head bent over more mending, the curtain of shiny brown hair half hiding her face, and he thought about how she had looked in bed early that morning.

"Camilla."

He took the sewing from her hands and pulled her to him. She started to say something to him, but he silenced her with a kiss that went on and on. He stretched out on the floor and pulled her down beside him, turning to fit her against his body. It was amost an hour before Camilla remembered to ask him about *his* Christmas traditions. She lay in his arms with her head on his chest, feeling the vibrations of his voice when he talked.

"I don't have any since I left home. We used to open presents on Christmas morning and have a big dinner, or a not-so-big dinner some years, although it always seemed pretty good. Since I left the family, I've spent Christmas with friends here and there all over the world. It isn't a bad way to spend the holiday," he said, assessing his life— something he had had time to do in the past few days. The more time he spent with Camilla, the more he learned about her. He saw she had an inner satisfaction that he envied. And his own life began to look frivolous, empty. He was constantly on the go, restless if he wasn't busy. But with her he felt as if he could lock them in the house, throw away the key, and still be happy. The knowledge amazed him. Each hour with her satisfied him completely. He knew one thing he wanted in his future as surely as he knew there was a sun in the sky—Camilla.

They were on the floor, their skin warmed by flames from the fire. Embers glowed brightly, and a log split, sending a shower of sparks racing up the chimney. She lay in the crook of his arm, her hair fanned across his chest.

"So what do you want to do Christmas morning? We don't have to be at the mission until eleven o'clock."

His thoughts were elsewhere. "Camilla, remember that picture in the paper of Sheryl?"

"Yes," she answered, suddenly coming out of her daze.

"Well, she isn't important now. She never was that important to me. No one seems that important to me any longer, except you. I love—"

She rolled over and placed her hand lightly on his mouth so he couldn't talk.

"Don't say things like that. You don't know how you'll feel when your life is back to normal. You don't have to tell me you love me. I'm happy, Ken. So happy to have had this time with you."

"Dammit, don't send me packing!"

She giggled. "I'm not sending you packing like this, sir! Talk about being arrested!"

He grinned and smoothed her hair away from her face. "Now, as I was saying . . ."

"Not another word on the subject," she ordered.

"You're getting damn bossy." His hand drifted down to feel the enticing curve of her tiny waist, the flare of her hip. She drew in her breath as she ran her fingers across his chest, tangling them in the soft mat of curls, and all teasing was gone as they loved each other.

She stirred first, shaking him. "Ken, we're going to be late."

He groaned and reached out for her, but she slipped away.

"Really late! I'm going to shower and dress while you wake up."

His gaze drifted down across her full breasts and lower, as he realized she was what he wanted, all he wanted, ever. "I can't hear you, Camilla," he said in a husky voice as his arousal came swiftly. "Come closer."

"You know I can't!" She turned and left, but he caught the quick flare of desire in her expression, and he was glad she was as lusty as he. In spite of her head start, he was ready minutes before she was. He went to the kitchen to get a drink of water, striding out of the room in his new jeans and gray sweater.

Just as she was pulling on her boots she heard the phone. When she answered it, she recognized Jesse Early's voice. Ken picked up the phone in the kitchen, and Camilla hung up to gather her muffler and knitted gloves. She paused in front of the mirror and wondered at the transformation she saw in herself.

To Ken's delight several of the people at the mission hadn't recognized her when she first appeared with her hair down. She didn't think she looked like the same person she was yesterday.

She felt aglow with love and happiness, and it seemed to show. She leaned forward and whispered, "Dear Kenneth Holloway, I love you!"

Humming a tune, she started for the door, realizing she hadn't noticed her scars at all.

"Camilla!" Ken shouted, and her heart lurched. Breathlessly, suddenly frightened over what might have happened, she ran back into the kitchen.

Eight

He scooped her up and swung her in a circle, laughing as he held her. "Maybe things are taking a turn for the better. That was Jesse, and he said the name I gave him was a hot lead."

"That's marvelous!"

Ken set her down. "He said he doesn't have any tangible evidence yet, but he thinks this is our guy. He wanted to know if I cared if he called the police and gave them an anonymous tip so they could start checking into it with all their resources."

"Oh, Ken, how wonderful!" she said, hugging him, feeling tears of relief sting her eyes.

"Hey, damn, do I see tears?"

He held her away, and she laughed and tried to brush the tears away quickly.

He crushed her to him. "Don't cry over good news. It's a waste of tears."

"I never heard of anyone wasting tears!" she said, trying to get control of her feelings.

"Lordy, I feel like a stone weight has been lifted off my shoulders! Hey, we're going to be late. Let's go."

She grabbed her parka and started to put it on, but he caught her and spun her back into his arms. "One last kiss," he said gruffly, and kissed her hard.

"Now we'll be late for sure."

When they reached the mission, they were too busy to talk to each other. Occasionally while she was working she would feel his hand squeeze her shoulder, or his fingers brush across her back. She would turn to catch a wink or a smile from him, enough to warm her more than the steamy kitchen.

People in need of food or shelter poured into the mission all afternoon. Sometime during late afternoon she noticed Ken was gone. She couldn't imagine where he could be and she was alarmed for a few minutes. Once she glanced outside to see if her car was still in the parking lot. Then later she saw Ken carrying a pan filled with steaming dressing. He winked at her, and she smiled, forgetting about his disappearance.

At midnight there was a brief candlelight ceremony and a prayer was said by a local minister who helped at the mission. As she knelt in prayer beside Ken she felt his hand close over hers. She held it tightly, locking her fingers in his, saying a silent prayer that he would be cleared of the crime.

Another storm had been predicted, and by twelve

o'clock, when they started for home, the first flakes were beginning to fall.

Ken held out his hand. "Just in time for Christmas. I like snow at Christmas." He dropped his arm across her shoulders. I've spent it in the tropics before, and it just isn't the same."

For an instant she thought about how different their lives were and how soon her idyll with him would end. Permanently. She shook her head. She would weather that storm as she had weathered others in her life. She wasn't a part of Ken's world, and she knew it to her bones. Never for a moment, no matter how much he had professed to love her, had she expected him to continue to feel that way later.

She began to sing a carol softly, and he joined her with his deep voice as they trudged through the snow to the car. They sang songs on the way home, and as soon as they stepped inside the kitchen door they fell into each other's arms.

Later as she was lying in his arms in front of the fire, she sighed with contentment.

Christmas. It was a time she had always loved, a time for reflecting on one's values, renewing ties with loved ones. This Christmas, when she had made a difficult decision to stay because they were shorthanded at the mission and she was so badly needed, had turned out to be the most glorious Christmas of all.

Presents from her family and her closest friends were under the tree, but it was Ken—who wouldn't be able to give her any material thing—who would make this Christmas the most special one ever.

She ran her hand across his chest down to his

flat stomach, and his arm tightened around her even though he seemed to be sound asleep.

Morning came, and they both stirred in bed, where they'd moved to late that night. "Merry Christmas, sleepyhead," Ken said drowsily. "Ready to open presents?"

"Mmm, maybe in a minute or two," she answered provocatively, trailing her fingers along his bare thigh beneath the covers.

"Or maybe next July," he said, rolling over, his weight coming down on top of her as he kissed her throat.

When they left the bedroom, she was wearing her quilted robe and Ken had on jeans and socks.

"Ken, I feel ridiculous opening my family's presents while you sit and watch."

"Don't be absurd. I have a mound of presents from my family, and someday you can watch me open them."

Her lashes lowered as she moved away quickly. Catching her arm, he turned her to face him. "Somehow I have the feeling you don't expect to be there to see me open my presents."

"It's Christmas. I want to give you a present. Come on," she said, avoiding his accusation and wishing he couldn't tell quite so easily what was in her thoughts.

"Okay," he said, dropping the matter, because he knew in his heart she would be there. He intended to see to it that she was. She was a marvel to him, and he was impatient to be free to do things for her. He was as excited now as he had been when he was a little kid. Christmas had always been nice, but the breathtaking excitement had vanished long ago. Until now. He couldn't wait to give her his present, and he felt like grinning from ear to ear.

She knelt to poke among the presents and pulled out one for Ken, handing it to him.

"Merry Christmas."

"Let me give you yours."

"In a second. I want to watch you open yours first."

He smiled and peeled away the red paper and white ribbon, tossing the box aside as he withdrew a paperweight. It had a snowman inside it, and he smiled as he looked at the figure a moment, then hugged her.

"I like it, and every time I look at it I'll remember our snowman."

"I thought you might."

"Now, my dear sexy lady, I have two presents for you—due to circumstances beyond my control." He leaned down and pulled out a package from beneath a mound she'd had stacked there for over a week.

It was wrapped in the Sunday funnies and tied with yellow yarn that he had probably found at the mission. She was delighted and couldn't imagine how he had gotten her any kind of present.

"When in the world did you get me a present?"

He caught her hands and stopped her, looking at her with such a solemn expression that her breath caught in her throat. "Don't expect much."

"I never do," she said matter-of-factly. "Remember?"

"Well, I'll have to do something about that, but I couldn't shop, and you know it. I got this from the guy that runs the garage and body shop, to use the term loosely."

"The garage and body shop by the mission?" she asked, turning the package in her hands, relishing the thought of Ken making such an effort for her. "That's where you disappeared to yesterday! I was worried about you."

"Sorry, but I couldn't tell you. Everything in the place is used, so you're getting secondhand goods," he said quietly, "but I wanted something you could remember this Christmas by."

Her throat tightened, and she worked the yarn free, expecting a snow scraper for the car or something useful, happy no matter what the gift might be.

She opened a battered box, and nestled in a wad of rumpled newspaper was a gleaming brass bell. She picked it up, shaking it and listening to it jingle.

"Oh, Ken, I love it! I'll keep it and remember this day always." She hugged him. "Where did you get it at that place? This doesn't go on a car."

"Hell, no. He had it hanging on his door as you enter the shop. I hid in the bathroom and polished it up for you with your brass polish!"

"Oh, thank you!" she cried, laughing and hugging him again.

"Lordy, you're easy to please, he said, captivated by her shining eyes. He had one brief mental picture of how he had intended to spend his Christmas with Sheryl in Switzerland. He was going to give her a diamond necklace, but he knew it wouldn't have brought the same sparkle to her eyes as his gift of the bell had brought to Camilla's. Then he forgot Sheryl as Camilla handed him a long flat box.

"Here's another for you."

He opened it quickly, ripping the green paper to shreds and pulling out a soft plaid cashmere muffler. "I like this," he said, experiencing a surge of joy that she had somehow managed the time to get him the gifts.

"I thought it would go with your topcoat."

He looked up from admiring the muffler. "My topcoat? You haven't seen it except those few minutes when you returned my wallet."

"I remember."

Ken scooped her up and carried her to the sofa, settling her on his lap. "I love you. Presents are inadequate, particularly my presents this morning," he added dryly.

"If you don't stop all this hugging and kissing," she said breathlessly, "we won't get to open the rest of the presents before we have to leave for the mission."

"Do tell. And you don't like all this hugging and kissing?"

"I'm not sure," she said with teasing caution. "Let's try again and I'll see."

"Anything to oblige a pretty lady," he answered cheerfully, and did oblige until she finally stopped him.

"I have one more present for you," she said, thinking how she had drawn out of her savings to get it. She prayed it was something he would like, because she knew so little about him.

He ripped through the paper as swiftly as he

had the others, and lifting the lid on the box, he took out the small bronze eagle in flight.

At the time it had seemed to be something he might like, but now as she waited she was filled with uncertainty.

"Ah, Camilla, how great!" he said, warmth filling his voice, and she knew instantly that he was pleased.

"I'm so glad."

He kissed her again, and finally she had to push him away. "Go fix some breakfast while I open my other presents. My family will call to ask me about them any minute now."

"I want to watch, so you hurry and open your presents, and then I'll fix breakfast," he said, amused because he couldn't recall a single woman he had ever dated who had ordered him to fix breakfast, lunch, or dinner. He tried to be patient, but anticipation was gnawing at him. He wanted to shove aside all her presents and give her his special one, but he wanted more to save what he hoped would be the best present until the last. He wanted her full attention when she opened it.

"I guess I'll do it your way," she said, tearing off the wrappings and showing him each thing. He smiled and gazed at her, his long legs stretched out, one hand resting casually on the bronze statue. He said "That's nice" to each thing until she opened her sister Lou's present.

"Ahh," he said, crossing the room to pull the filmy, lacy pink nightgown out of the box. "Now, I call this a Christmas present!" He held it up. "When can I see it modeled?"

She snatched it out of his hands. "Later, later! Let me get through here before they call."

He kissed her and sat down, smiling contentedly. As she continued to open presents and they talked, she learned he had borrowed money from Will, one of the volunteer workers at the mission, to buy the bell from the shop owner.

Finally she sat in a mound of torn paper and ribbon, her presents neatly stacked behind her.

"Oh, Ken, I wish you had your presents here."

"This is better. You forgot—"

The phone interrupted him, and she jumped up. "It's my family," she said hurrying to the kitchen.

He followed and began to get breakfast ready while she chatted with her mother, then her father, and in turn, each of the nieces and nephews who were old enough to talk. She thanked each one, listened to their thanks in return, and finally her mother was on the line again.

Ken placed a cup of hot coffee in front of her. She sipped the coffee, and in a short time he put a plate of crisp bacon and golden eggs in front of her, brushing her cheek with a kiss and letting his hand drift across her back.

"I'm fine, really," Camilla said. "I know, I'd like to be there, but they need me so badly at the mission, and we'll all be together in March, and you and Dad will be here in April. I'm all right. Really, I am, and I'm not alone. I have a friend with me, and we're having a good time. My friend is alone for Christmas too. I love you too. I love all of you and I'll write. I'll call in a few days, Mom. What? Oh, a friend who works with me at the mission. Bye." She replaced the receiver, and he came across the room and took her arm, leading her back to the tree.

"Too chicken to tell them your friend is a male, weren't you?"

"Yes," she said with a laugh. "And you ought to be glad I was. Otherwise I'd be on the phone answering questions for the next hour."

"No, you wouldn't. We don't have that much time."

"Thanks for the breakfast. You're a pretty good cook."

"Pretty good? I'm going to be the fastest potato peeler in the West if I keep going to the mission with you!"

"What are we doing?" she asked as he stopped in front of the tree and looked at her expectantly.

"You forgot a present."

Surprised, she looked at the base of the tree. "Well, where is it? I don't see one."

"Look on the tree."

It took her a minute to spot a tiny little wad of comic-strip paper tied with ordinary white string. She laughed and picked it off the tree, wondering what could possibly be inside such a tiny package. It looked as if it only held a thumbtack or a dime.

Again he stopped her. "Camilla, that's only a substitute. I got that at the mission."

The phone rang and he swore. "Dammit to hell."

"I'll get it. Probably one of my friends." They hurried to the kitchen and she picked up the phone, then she handed the receiver to him. "It's Jesse."

Ken snatched the phone, and she started to open the small package. His hand closed over hers, stopping her, and she realized he wanted her to wait until he had hung up.

"Yeah?" He suddenly closed his eyes. "Thank God," he said so fervently, her heart lurched, and she knew he had been cleared of the crime. Something must have turned up to shift the blame from him. She held her breath, praying that she was right.

He covered the mouthpiece. "They got the man. The hired killer. And he's talked this morning. Evidence and all. It was Moreland who did it for the inheritance." He turned back to the phone. "Yeah, yeah. I'll call Chief Leonard. Of course. You send whatever bill you want to send! Yeah. That's the best news I've ever had! I'll call you at nine in the morning. Sure. Thanks, Jesse. Thanks more than I can tell you. I don't care what your bill is!"

He replaced the phone, and she threw her arms around him. "The man confessed in detail. Oh, Lord, what a relief! I've got to call Chief Leonard, but I'll do it from a pay phone on our way into town."

"Ken, I'm so glad! What a wonderful Christmas present."

"That's an understatement! I'm free. Jesse has talked to my attorney and he's already talked with Chief Leonard."

"How did they catch him?"

"I don't know any of the details. All I know is that it's over, and I'm in the clear. I can walk around a free man. I think I have a new appreciation for life." He smiled at her. "Everything's okay, so let's turn our thoughts to more important matters. Open your present."

"More important matters?" she echoed with a laugh, unwrapping the paper. For the first few seconds she was completely at a loss, wondering if it was a token gift. She stared at a worn ring with a blue glass stone that looked as if it came from the five-and-dime store. The brass band was green in a spot, and one prong was bent; Camilla was puzzled.

Ken waited, holding his breath until she raised her head. She looked at him in bewilderment, and he realized she didn't have the slightest idea what it signified.

"Damn, you meant it when you said you never expected anything, didn't you?" he said with amazement, then took the ring and slid it on her finger. "Will you marry me?"

Nine

Shocked, Camilla stared at him. He leaned down, his face coming closer.

"I love you. I want you to be my wife. Will you marry me?"

"I don't know," she said, too stunned to think. She wanted to fling herself into his arms and shout yes, yes, yes, but she hadn't expected a proposal. Never once had she considered the possibility that he would ask her to marry him. All she could do was look at him.

"It's too fast, Ken, for you to be sure," Camilla said solemnly, trying to keep a grip on her emotions.

"I know," he said in a manner that sent a ripple coursing through her. She was a cautious, sensible person, and never for one second had she seen herself as a part of Ken's life in the future. And she couldn't do so now.

"We can't marry when we've known each other for so short a time."

Her answer hit him like ice water, and he realized for once in his life he was out of his depth with a woman. "I love you."

"You don't know how you'll feel when things return to normal. Ken, I don't fit into your world. I don't even know it. You're part of the jet set. I work at a mission."

"That doesn't mean we don't love each other and can't adjust. Dammit, I adjusted to the mission. You ought to be able to adjust to 'my world' as you call it."

"This is a surprise."

"So I see. I believed your statements of love, Camilla, and I do expect things. I expect the world and all," he said, and his voice was hard as steel. Suddenly his eyes narrowed. "Maybe I just didn't go about this the right way." He caught her up, crushing the breath out of her lungs as he hugged her and kissed her until she forgot the ring.

Camilla held him, her heart pounding, desire sweeping through her like a tidal wave.

He raised his head. "Give me a chance, will you? Give us one before you refuse?"

"Of course," she whispered, holding him, for the first time daring to think of herself as a permanent part of his life.

"Does this mean yes?"

"I'm not sure I can think straight until you let go of me," she said, running her hands across his bare shoulders, feeling the hard muscles, his smooth, warm skin.

"I might not ever let go of you," he said roughly,

not a trace of teasing in his voice. "Okay, Camilla. Don't wear the silly old ring, but I'm not getting out of your life until you throw me out."

A sense of panic buffeted her. She was tossed into a stormy world she didn't know. She was unsure, unable to believe he truly loved her, yet she couldn't refuse. She wanted him too badly. "You don't mind if it's sort of a tentative engagement?"

Suddenly he grinned, and his voice became more gentle and husky. "No, I don't mind a bit if I'm 'sort of' engaged. Suits me just fine."

His lightness didn't match her feelings, because she still didn't dare hope it could work out, and she knew him well enough to know patience wasn't one of his virtues.

"Ken, I saw the picture of Sheryl in the paper. She's on the covers of national magazines. I'm sure she's sophisticated; she's breathtakingly beautiful, wealthy—things I'm not. And while you may not love her, she's the type of woman you're accustomed to. This incident is a brief moment in your life blown all out of proportion. You're in shock—you won't feel the same when everything settles down. I'll be Millie Blake, school dietitian and Sunshine Mission volunteer."

"Camilla Blake, you are the most delightful, wonderful woman I have ever known," he said quietly. "Can you guess how bored I sometimes get with Sheryl? No, you can't."

"You can't get that bored if you were going to spend Christmas in Switzerland with her."

"Why do you think I chose to go to Switzerland? I can ski there and we have lots of friends. How long would I last shut up like this with Sheryl? Or Sheryl with me? If I had given her a secondhand bell that had come from the door of an old run-down body shop—"

Camilla didn't know if it was hysteria or comic relief, but she had to laugh. He grinned and hugged her.

"Stop all the nonsense and trust me, Miss Usually-Ever-So-Trustful!"

She laughed as she looked at the ring. "This is absolutely the most beautiful ring I've ever seen."

"You're gong to be late to the mission," he whispered in her ear, his breath tickling her, "but if you're going to be six minutes late, why not make it ten?"

She tried to wriggle out of his grasp. "Stop! It won't be ten if you keep that up." Her laughter faded when she saw his smoldering expression and knew how badly he wanted her. She walked into his arms again.

"It might as well be ten or twenty or even thirty. I've never been late before. I'm entitled."

"Baby, are you ever!"

As they drove to town she watched trees whip past. They skidded slightly and Ken instantly righted the car, then continued on down the mountain to the highway. Wind buffeted the vehicle, and shadows were long and purple across the snow because the sun had already dropped to a low angle in the western sky.

As the car skidded briefly again Camilla explained, "You'll get arrested for speeding before you can turn yourself in of your own free choice!" she studied the ring, then looked at him, something she felt she would like to do every minute for eternity. He was dressed again in the suit, tie, and white shirt he had worn the night of the murder, and even though the clothes were slightly rumpled, he had an air of elegance and command about him that was unmistakable.

"I don't want you to be any later than necessary, and I'm going a little out of the way."

"Whatever you say," she said blissfully.

"When you answer me like that, I want to turn this car around and head right back to your place."

She ran her hand along his thigh, feeling the warmth of his flesh through the soft wool. "Whatever makes you feel that way?" she asked in a sultry voice.

"Dammit! If you don't stop, back we go."

She laughed and scooted to her side of the car while she studied the scenery again. The last remnants of sunshine glittered on the snowy landscape. The diamond-bright dazzle of snow crystals matched the sparkle she felt over Ken. Yet there was no way she could get rid of the deep, strong conviction he would soon feel differently about her, and she seesawed between joy and worry. After a few more minutes he stopped the car on a deserted downtown street and turned to her.

"We're about two blocks from the police station. I'll get out here and walk so no one will know where I've been until our engagement hits the papers, and people put two and two together."

"Our engagement." She couldn't accept the fact that she was actually engaged to him. And she couldn't treat the moment lightly. In spite of his promises and lovemaking and the secondhand ring, she knew she was losing him.

"Kenneth Holloway, I love you," she whispered, placing her hands on his cheeks. "And I always will. Always. You are my first, only, and last great love. I know that, just like I know I like movies and castles and oceans."

"Oh, Lord!" he ground out the words as he stepped out of the car.

For a moment she was dismayed that he hadn't kissed her good-bye, and then her heart lurched when she saw he was coming around the car. He yanked open the door and pulled her out, squeezing the breath from her in a hug.

"I love you, Camilla! I'll call you as soon as I'm free from the police."

"Okay, Ken," she said, fighting back tears, sure to her toes that things weren't going to work out the way he expected.

"You're damn trusting of ninety-nine percent of things dealing with people and life, but on the future, you're a total pessimist."

"I'm just practical. Practical clothes, practical outlook, practical life . . ."

"Sure," he said dryly. "Practical lovemaking. Standard, ordinary . . ."

Her humor surfacing, she ran her hand along his thigh to the bulge in his slacks. "Ordinary?"

"Dammit! Want me to haul you into a dark alley? You'll get us arrested!"

She laughed and leaned away, her worries momentarily vanquished. She shook her head, the heavy strands of brown hair swinging behind her shoulders.

"Be careful," she said, knowing it was good-bye no matter what he said.

"Don't worry. Everything's okay now. I'll call you tonight."

She raised her lips for his kiss, clinging to him, wanting to hold the moment forever in her memory, because his proposal and promises were bubbles that could burst at any time. The wind caught locks of his dark hair, blowing them back from his face.

"Stop holding me like we'll never kiss again!" he said roughly. "You'll be in my arms tomorrow and tomorrow and tomorrow!"

"I don't even know what kind of house you live in, what hobbies you have—"

"You will!" he said, releasing her. "And we'll have our own house, not mine or yours! I better start walking before some squad car comes along and picks me up. And boy, are you late for work! Tell Joel I'll talk to him. He'll get a reward. So will the other two for their help."

"Bye, Ken. Take care."

"It isn't good-bye, Camilla," he said solemnly. "I'm smart enough to know what I want."

"Sure."

"See you tonight or tomorrow," he called over his shoulder, jamming his hands into his pockets. He hunched his shoulders against the brisk, cold wind and headed for the police station.

She climbed into her car and drove to the mission, where she became too busy serving dinner and cleaning up afterward to think about anything else. Except, even in the midst of a crowd, she missed Ken.

Late that night when she returned home, she heard the phone ringing and when she picked up the receiver, she heard Ken's familiar baritone. "Hi, beautiful!"

She laughed, her pulse jumping while she reveled in the sound of his deep voice. "Tell me everything. I just came in the door."

"Lordy, have I been busy! My hotel suite is full of people. I'm in the bedroom trying to get a moment of privacy. What's your schedule at the mission?"

"I don't have to work after next Tuesday, because I wanted to give myself a brief vacation."

"Any chance you can cancel tomorrow so we can go out Saturday night?"

"Yes. I can work it out."

"Good. I'll see you—" He broke off to answer someone else in the room and in seconds he was back. His voice softened, a subtle drop in tone that sent a tingle through her.

"Six o'clock. Okay?"

"Six?" she asked, startled at the early hour.

"I have a party I'm obligated to attend before we go out to eat. I'd like you to go with me. All right?"

"Of course."

His voice dropped another notch. "I can't believe how much I miss you!"

"Keep telling me," she said dreamily, stretching out on the sofa. "Now I have to go to bed alone after being in your arms every night."

He groaned and then turned away to answer

someone else. "Camilla, I have to go talk to a reporter and to my attorney and to too many people."

"At this hour?"

"I was at the police station until nine o'clock. It's been wild ever since I walked in the door. Look, hon, I want to have lunch with you tomorrow. Do you have the afternoon free too?"

"Yes, I do," she answered breathlessly, delighted she would see him during the day as well as that night.

"Good. I'll pick you up at noon." His voice became raspy. "I love you. The minute you say yes, I want our engagement to end. I want the wedding to be soon."

A cold touch of panic clutched at her heart when she thought about how swiftly he was rushing into marriage. "You have to be sure, Ken."

"*I have to be?* I am sure."

"I don't believe it quite yet. I don't think I'll fit in, and someday, I'm afraid you'll think so too."

"Will you stop that? I wish I could kiss you. That always ends your foolishness! Noon. I'll pick you up. Honey, I'm afraid your name is going to be in the papers soon as the woman who hid me from the police."

"I don't care about that as long as they don't come to arrest me!"

He chuckled. "Don't worry. They won't. Chief Leonard is a nice fellow. Very understanding. Gotta run," he said, but his words slowed and his voice was a husky whisper. "But, oh, how I'd like to kiss you all over just like I did this morning. Remember?"

She felt as if she were on fire, her body remembering as much as her mind, responding to his sexy tone, reacting to the furry warmth of his deep voice. Without realizing it, she moaned softly.

"How I wish you were here right now. Noon, hon." The phone clicked, and they were cut off. She replaced the receiver in the cradle and lay with her eyes closed, relishing each precious memory, praying she would fit into his life because she adored him.

Saturday at noon when she opened the door, Ken stood for a moment and just looked at her. He took in her violet sweater and pastel plaid wool skirt, and she looked with equal intensity at him. He was dressed casually in brown wool slacks that fit flawlessly and a tan sweater, and he looked more handsome than ever. Her heart thudded with eagerness as she walked into his arms. An hour later he asked her to dress because he had an appointment. She stretched and smiled languidly, wanting to stay in bed with him.

"How'd you get the super tan?" she asked, looking at his muscles as he gathered his clothes.

He grinned. "On beaches. You'll get one, too, on our honeymoon. How does a very private, sunny beach sound?"

She couldn't answer, because she knew he wasn't listening to her protests about rushing into marriage.

"Honeymoon, Camilla! Start getting used to the idea."

She smiled to prevent an argument, but worry still plagued her.

As soon as he was dressed again, he went out to the car. She showered and decided to put on lacy underthings, and stepped into the bedroom to get the rest of her clothes. Ken was sitting in a chair, waiting for her. His gaze lowered, lingering as he looked at her bare legs.

He stood up. "We have to run errands, but I don't really want to go. I'd rather stay here with you." He picked up a large box wrapped in shiny red paper, tied with an elegant gold bow. "Now, I can do this right," he said, handing her the package. "Merry Christmas."

"Oh, Ken, I love the bell and the ring. You didn't need to buy me another present!"

She carefully began to remove the wrapping while he fidgeted. "Why don't you tear the ribbon off? If I'd known it would take this long, I wouldn't have had them wrap the thing!"

She laughed and tore the paper and ribbon, feeling excitement bubble up within her. When she raised the lid, she gasped and stared at the present.

"Ken, I can't accept this!"

He pulled the full-length dark mink coat from the box. "Don't tell me about the little minks who've lost their lives. This one time you can make an exception. Put it on for me."

Her protests died when she looked into his eyes, and she slipped her arms into the sleeves, feeling the cool satin lining against her arms and legs, running her hand over the soft, luxurious fur.

She couldn't talk, not because of the coat, but because of all it represented.

"Thank you," she said, hugging him.

"This goes with it." He held out a box and opened it to reveal a sparkling diamond ring. "Give me your hand."

He removed the old ring, replaced it with the diamond, and then he kissed her. Joyous, she wrapped her arms around his neck and returned his kisses, forgetting all her worries.

"Next stop, Cosley's." He said the name of an exclusive shop in their area. "I want to get you a dress for the holidays, and I don't want to hear a protest from you."

"No, sir."

"That's good. And I have a few other things in mind. I want to make up for not having anything new to give you on Christmas, and don't tell me I don't need to."

She didn't.

While they were riding down the mountain to the highway she asked him, "Tell me what happened. Did Alan Moreland confess?"

"Yes," Ken said, his voice serious. The hired gun was a guy by the name of Dutch Chaney. I didn't tell you the name before because I thought the less you knew, the safer you'd be. Maybe it's an alias. He told all, because they found some of Walter's things in his possession and they found my wallet in his car."

"Oh, I'm so glad it isn't flimsy evidence!"

"He told the police how a man by the name of Moore contacted him, but it was Alan. They had enough to go on to bring Alan in for questioning, and Dutch Chaney identified him as the man who had hired him for the job. Alan confessed. From what I understand, he said he was to inherit everything. Then after Walter's health problems became serious and he faced a terminal illness, Walter began to have a change of heart about what he had done to me."

She stroked Ken's arm, hoping he had lost all the animosity he had felt toward Walter when she first met him. He patted her hand, then wound his fingers through hers.

"Walter must have had a change of temperament as well as a change of heart. I suspect he figured I would take better care of him than Alan if something happened and he couldn't run his own affairs. And he wanted me to have the company. I guess blood is thicker than water, as the old saying goes. Anyway, Walter must have acquired some scruples during his illness. He thought it only fair to tell Alan he was changing his will. Alan is ambitious and ruthless, and he didn't want to give all that up to some squirt kid who used to get in his hair."

She laughed. "A squirt kid," she repeated, thinking how handsome and commanding and powerful Ken was.

"I was, back then," he said.

"I doubt if you ever were," she said dryly. "Go on."

"Alan didn't think Walter was being fair to him after he had devoted years to the company, and I had fought the old man all the way. Half the time Walter probably enjoyed the battles. Alan convinced Walter to wait and think about it before he acted.

Walter agreed, and that's when Alan got busy planning the murder."

"How terrible! I'm so glad they found out about him."

"Well, it was thanks to you, my pretty lady. First we'll look at dresses and I'll watch while you model for me. Then a black lace nightgown—"

"What?"

He grinned, and she saw he had been teasing.

Later that night at the party she glanced at her image in a long gilt mirror on a wall of the elegant room, and she was reassured as far as her appearance was concerned.

She wore the simple black woolen dress Ken had selected that afternoon. He had insisted on showering her with gifts. He told her he had sent a donation to the mission, and she suspected it was enormous. He had provided her with thick sealed envelopes to give to Will, Joel, Murph, and Barney.

She felt transformed; Ken was changing, too, the worry and tenseness no longer plaguing him. He was more assertive, quicker to laugh, but he was also slightly more remote, caught up in the endless details about his business that had been neglected while he was in hiding.

With another glance in the mirror she thought she looked as if she fit into the party, but she didn't *feel* as if she fit. She wore makeup tonight— mascara, powder, a slight bit of blush on her cheeks, and a touch of shadow—and she was more than satisfied with the way she looked and thrilled with Ken's attention. But so often in the course of conversation she was lost because she didn't know any of the people's names or anything about their companies. She hadn't traveled to Europe—or anywhere out of the United States. She and Ken were both younger than almost everyone else, and she was keenly aware of her lack of experience in so many areas.

Camilla hadn't realized the extent of Ken's wealth and power before, and it awed her. He was a young man who had become enormously successful, and it was obvious he had an extremely bright, busy future ahead of him. She felt that he needed a wife with a similar background, someone who was as worldly, sophisticated, and poised as he was. And as attractive. At the moment Ken was occupied with several businessmen who had drawn him aside. She didn't mind being alone, but worries wouldn't stop buzzing through her mind.

"Ah, a lovely lady all alone," a man said, and stopped in front of her to offer his hand. "I'm Wesley Borden, a friend of Ken's. Actually an enemy. We play tennis together and he's a deadly foe."

"I'm Ca—"

"You're his lovely new fiancée," Wesley Borden said, admiring her ring before he released her hand. "What a lucky man! And you hid him away all last week," he said with open curiosity.

A slender brunette left a group of people and joined them. "Tell us about hiding Ken. I'm Ginger Oldfield. And I know you're Camilla Blake. Of course, if Ken Holloway knocked on my door as a stranger and asked me to take him in, I would have without hesitation."

"Of course, you would, and so would I," another feminine voice said, and their circle became larger.

"What did you do?" Ginger asked.

"Actually you ought to ask Ken. The week is a blur to me. In some ways it's like a dream," Camilla said pleasantly, and Wesley Borden laughed.

"She's not telling. Smart lady. Eat your heart out, ladies," he said under his breath to Camilla.

Ken looked across the room at Camilla while he listened to John Marks, his attorney, talk about Colorado's economy. His pulse skipped a beat as he spotted her in a circle of people. He thought she looked achingly beautiful, and he longed to get away from the party and be alone with her. She had changed him. He had always considered material things to be so important, and they held little value to her. He didn't know when he had started to see life through her eyes. Values had become important to him. And he was going to learn how to be patient!

"Think so, Ken?"

"Sorry, I didn't hear," he said quietly, turning his gaze from Camilla back to the group of men.

As the hour passed, people seemed to make a special effort to talk to her, and she knew they were more than mildly curious about her only because of Ken.

Later when Camilla was separated from him again, she wandered into the library to get away from the crowd. A fire was burning and the paneling and books made the room cozy. It was quiet and restful after meeting so many new people, and Camilla roamed around the room reading book titles. As she looked at various books she heard the click of heels in the hall and turned to see who it was.

A willowy auburn-haired woman in an emerald-green dress passed, glancing through the open door at Camilla. In seconds the woman returned, coming into the room and holding out her hand to shake Camilla's.

"I'm Gail Webb," she said, tossing her head so her page-boy–styled hair swung away from her face.

"I'm Camilla Blake."

"I know. I've wanted to meet you, but you were always across the room. I saw you standing in here alone. Where's Ken?"

"Talking business I guess," Camilla replied, suddenly feeling very conscious of her scars.

"I'm sure he is!" Gail exclaimed with a laugh while her curious gaze went over Camilla, stopping at her hand. "What a beautiful ring."

"Thank you," Camilla said politely, nervously holding her hand out so Gail could see the ring better.

She smiled. "I wanted to meet the woman Ken plans to marry. You're very lucky," she said, her voice full of mocking amusement.

"I think so too," Camilla answered, wondering how important Gail Webb had been to Ken in the past.

"Rumor is, you let him hide at your house, and he fell in love with you."

Camilla smiled and shrugged. "That's a nice rumor."

"There you are!" Ken said from the doorway, coming into the room. He was more handsome than ever in his flawless dark suit and white shirt. Tonight his unruly curls were combed into neat waves.

"I take it you two have met," he said easily. "How are you, Gail?"

"Fine. Congratulations, Ken."

"Thanks," he said, dropping his arm around Camilla's shoulders and giving her a squeeze. "Are you spending the holidays at home this year?"

"No, I leave tomorrow for the South, but it's been fun to stick around this long. Have you seen Phil yet?"

"No."

"He'll want to hear in great detail about your escapade. You've become notorious."

"It's over now." He looked down at Camilla. "We need to go. Are you ready?"

"Yes. It was nice to meet you, Gail."

"My pleasure. My best to you both. Congratulations again, Ken," she said, and swiftly kissed his cheek. "You shouldn't leave so early."

"Have to," Ken said with a shrug as all three of them entered the hall.

"Is the wedding date set?"

Ken looked at Camilla. "It's up to Camilla. Whenever she gives me a date, that's it."

Gail's brows arched, and Camilla saw the quick flash of surprise in her expression. Gail laughed. "So, Kenneth Holloway, is it possible that you've fallen in love?"

"Yes," he said happily, giving Camilla another squeeze, and for the first time in an hour, Camilla felt warm with pleasure.

Gail laughed. "Bye. I'll leave you two to your-selves!"

"Let's find our host and hostess to say good-bye, and we can go," Ken said, steering Camilla through the crowd of people in the living room.

"How do you know so many people?"

"I went to high school here and I worked for Walter, remember? And I've been back and forth all through the years, especially lately."

Inside his black Lincoln he pulled her close to him. In spite of the fur coat and the heater she felt chilled.

"We're off now to my favorite restaurant. I hope you like it—Louie's Cajun Bayou . . . Creole cooking."

"Yum," she said. "It happens to be my favorite too."

"No kidding? See, we have so many things in common—drinking coffee, building snowmen, eat-ing at Louie's, our love of books and the sea."

"I didn't know you loved the sea," she said, becoming aware again of how little she knew about him.

"What's wrong?" he asked as he slowed for a red light.

"Ken, I don't think you've given yourself time to know what you really want." She repeated the argument that was coming up more and more often. Each time she had a feeling he wasn't really hearing what she was trying to say.

"I don't know the people you know or the people anyone at the party was talking about. You're a very busy, powerful man, and you meet all kinds of sophisticated, beautiful women. We're poles apart, and I feel that sometime soon you'll come to your senses and think so too."

"Camilla, if you marry me, you'll know those same people," he said patiently.

"You make it sound so simple," she said, not reassured by his quick answer, but she dropped the subject.

The restaurant was crowded and noisy, the piano music drowning out some of the buzz of conversation and clink of dishes as waitresses in green gingham dresses and green-coated waiters hurried back and forth from the kitchen. A smiling host greeted him.

"Good evening, Mr. Holloway. Your table is ready."

"Fine, Ted," Ken said, and chatted with him as he escorted them to a table in a dark corner. The odor of frying fish and hot bread assailed Camilla as she sat down and looked at Ken across the dark wooden table. Candlelight flickered between them, making shadows dance across his handsome features, and all she wanted to do was go home, where she could be alone with him. He reached across the table to take her hand, and when she looked into his eyes she lost all her doubts and fears.

"Your dress is pretty; you look beautiful tonight."

"Thank you. Thank you for the dress."

"I want to give you the world," he said, rubbing his thumb across her knuckles. "And see the sparkle in your eyes like you had when you looked at the old brass bell."

"I love that brass bell."

"We'll build a home here wherever you like,"

Ken said. "But it will have to wait until summer. With everything that's happened this past week, work has piled up unbelievably—"

"Ken!"

He looked up, then stood to shake hands with a man and his wife. He introduced the couple to Camilla. For a moment the two men talked about trucks, and then the couple left and Ken sat back down.

"Next time I'm going to tell Ted I want a table in the *remotest* corner."

"As they said at the party tonight, you've become notorious."

"You better think about where you'd like to go for a honeymoon," he said in a husky voice, his gaze peeling away the black dress as he looked at her.

"Here comes the waiter," she said, her voice breathless from Ken's smoldering glance. "We better decide right now on dinner."

"I'm having my favorite—" He paused and arched his brows at her. "What's your favorite creole dish?"

"Jambalaya." They said it in unison and they both laughed.

"See? We're meant for each other," he said.

The jambalaya was thick, spicy, and delicious, but all she could see was Ken, and both of them left half their dinners untouched.

Back at her house he built a fire. "How beautiful you are," he said in his deep voice as he drew her closer to kiss her. After a moment he whispered in her ear. "Know why I picked this dress today as the one I liked best?"

"Mmm," she answered, more interested in kissing his throat.

"Because of this zipper," he whispered, tugging it down from the neck to inches below her waist. He shoved it off her shoulders and leaned back to look at the brief black bikini panties and lacy black bra he had given her earlier. She reached out to caress him, aching to kiss him again. Her heart thudded as he enveloped her in a crushing embrace that shut out everything else.

In bed hours later uncertainties crowded into her thoughts.

"What's wrong, Camilla?" he asked, his voice clear in the silence.

"Ken, can we just avoid hurrying into marriage? You're used to getting what you want in life, but this may be one time you're rushing in and making a mistake."

"Are you afraid you won't love me after we marry?"

"Great grief, no!" She sat up abruptly, the sheet falling around her waist, but she was oblivious of her nudity because her mind was on their problems. "Don't you understand what I've been saying? I'm afraid you won't love me! You'll be shackled with a woman who is rather plain in every way, and one day you may wake up and wish you had married someone else. I may be able to survive our parting now, but I won't later. For the moment I haven't expected or dared hope for more of you," she said quietly. "But if we marry, and then you realize what a mistake you made, I couldn't get over the hurt. Not ever."

"That's absurd."

"You know I'm shy. I can't suddenly stop being shy. It was difficult for me at that party tonight."

"All you have to be is the nice person you are at the mission. I didn't see any shyness there."

"I don't have the background to be sophisticated and cosmopolitan. But I'm not worried about that as much as I'm afraid you don't truly love me." When she saw his frown, she spoke quickly. "I can't believe that someday you won't take a long, good look at me, or see some woman more your type. Ken, those women I met were so beautiful."

"Will you stop that!" he said gruffly. "You're gorgeous. You're still a little shy because of faded scars that don't matter."

"Just give us time," she pleaded, thinking he had always turned a deaf ear to her suggestion that seemed so logical and important to her.

"I'm not rushing. If I'd had my way, we would have married yesterday and it wouldn't have been too soon for me! The whole problem is in your own mind, Camilla," he said gently, the irritation leaving his voice, "not in me. I know what I want, and I want to get married soon. I'm backed up with work because of the interference these last weeks, and now Walter's estate and the new business will occupy a lot of my attention. I'd like to take all the time you need and court you, but hon, I can't. All I can do is try to reassure you that I do know my own feelings."

His gaze swept over her and his voice softened. "I guess I'll just have to convince you that I love you enough to want to be with you the rest of my life," he said with teasing resignation, as if he faced a monumental chore. "What a task!" He reached out to caress her throat, his hand slipping lower to touch her bare breasts, and the argument and her fears were forgotten.

Tuesday night Camilla flew to Dallas with Ken to attend a party. He showed her his condo, a two-story red brick structure behind a high brick—and—wrought-iron wall with security guards on duty at the gate. The interior was done in shades of blue, and his bedroom was enormous. She stood looking at the floor-to-ceiling glass doors that opened onto a balcony and at the large king-size bed. "Don't you get lost in here?" she asked. "This one room is as big as my whole house!"

"I shared a room with two little brothers all my life until I moved in with Walter. I like plenty of room, peace and quiet, and privacy."

He said it with feeling, and she turned to look at him, catching a glimpse of a different man.

He shed his coat and crossed the room to wrap his arms around her. "I'll show you around in a while," he said in a husky voice.

"Make it a long while," she whispered.

The next day he had a business meeting, but they had dinner together. The following day they returned to Colorado. For the weekend and New Year's Eve they flew to Kansas City, where he had his home and headquarters. His house was an old Colonial set back behind oaks, and as Camilla rode up the driveway she couldn't picture herself in the house or imagine Ken living there.

"What do you do all alone in such a big house?"

"I've dreamed of 'such a big house' for so many years of my life, it's still wonderful to me. I love this house and I hope you will too. I'll move to Denver soon though. We'll pick out a house together or build one, but I want a big one. I don't need to ask if you want children. I know the answer."

"I don't even know how *you* feel about children. Do you want them?"

"Yes," he answered solemnly, squeezing her hand. He turned off the car motor in front of a three-car garage. "I have a housekeeper, Maggie Kline, but she's not working tonight. I wanted to be alone with you."

She waited while Ken got their suitcases out of the car. He was wearing a shearling coat over his jeans and gray sweater, and western boots. His rugged clothing complemented his handsome features.

Inside the house Camilla walked on a deep cream-colored carpet through rooms she already knew had been done by an interior decorator. The furnishings were as elegant as the house: oil paintings, antiques, an oak-paneled den with brown leather couches. She scanned the room while Ken started a fire.

He showed her his bedroom, which was bigger than the one in his Dallas condo. It was filled with stereo equipment, a large desk, and a king-size bed. The decor was deep blue and white with red accents. Attractive as well as practical, the room was filled with plants and bookshelves that held Ken's trophies for swimming and tennis. A gun rack was stocked with rifles, and as she moved around quietly she began to learn more about him, but she also felt the gulf between them widening.

The kitchen had a rustic, inviting look to it. It had oak cabinets and woodwork and a large fireplace in one corner. As she watched Ken pour glasses of white wine for them she remembered how he had worked in the mission kitchen, and it seemed as if he were a different person.

"Why the frown?" he asked as he handed her a glass.

"I was thinking about you at the mission and you in your own kitchen. The images don't fit together."

"I'm one and the same guy. I can peel potatoes here as well as I did there," he said lightly. "Let's go where we'll be more comfortable."

The phone interrupted them and while he answered it she went into the den and sat in front of the fire. Her gaze swept over the leather furniture and the artwork on the walls. He was far more successful than she had guessed, and now he would inherit all of Walter Poplin's estate. It overwhelmed her. Mentally she couldn't fit Ken into her family, into her life at all in spite of the brief, glorious time they'd had together. And she still couldn't see herself in his world.

He was busier than she had imagined. How could she marry him and then constantly be saying good-bye? She wouldn't be able to continue working as a dietitian, because she knew from what he had said to her that he would expect her to travel with him some of the time. She wanted a family, and she wanted her children's father to be home with them a reasonable amount of the time. But deep down she couldn't really accept the fact that Ken truly loved her. He was an aggressive, competitive man and had been that way all his life; everything about him—his houses, his businesses, his trophies—attested to his drive and ambition. Perhaps her reluctance, instead of his love, was giving him the impetus to pursue her simply because she was a challenge to him.

"Camilla," he said from the doorway, and the moment she looked at him, she knew something was wrong.

Ten

He came down two steps into the room, the thick beige carpet muffling his steps. "I'm sorry. I have to leave. My asphalt plant in Dallas is on fire."

"Oh, no!"

"Oh, yes, unfortunately. I hope whoever made up the saying that trouble comes in threes is wrong. I'm flying down there, and two of my men are going with me. Will you come along?"

"You go. I'll stay here."

"You can come if you want. There's room on the plane."

"No, you go."

"I'll come back as soon as possible. Do you mind waiting here?"

"No," she said, genuinely concerned and sorry about the trouble Ken was having.

"I'll call. Come upstairs and talk to me while I pack."

She went upstairs with him, but he ended up

spending most of the time on the phone, and they had little conversation. She helped him pack as much as she could, and in less than a quarter of an hour, he was kissing her good-bye at the back door.

"I showed you the burglar system, and there are numbers by the phone if you need anyone. I hate to leave you."

"Go on. The sooner you go, the sooner you'll be back."

She watched him stride to the car, climb in, and slam the door, and she wondered again if she could adjust to constantly having to say good-bye to him. She wanted a family, and she wanted a husband who didn't have to divide his time between three homes and travel.

She sighed and closed the door. The large kitchen suddenly seemed to empty.

It was only an hour until the New Year's Eve party they were supposed to attend when Ken returned. From that moment on, the rest of the week was delightful. But on Monday she went back to work, Ken flew to Dallas, and she had to face reality. It was as painful as she had expected. They were separated constantly because of his travels; he was busy with Walter's estate as well as his own concerns.

And she noticed subtle changes in him. He called less and less often. He was more abrupt when they talked on the phone. He was gone more than he was in Denver, and their time together became shorter. As the days passed she began to feel forlorn. She didn't want to share bits and pieces of his life. She knew it was absurd to hope he would change; the future was still something she couldn't foresee. It was impossible to picture herself married to Ken.

Friday night she was in Denver with him, but they had a party to attend. On Saturday they finally were alone, and she decided to confront him as they sat near the fire in each other's arms. The woolly smell of his blue shirt mingled with the odor of an enticing after-shave, and she leaned her head back against his shoulder. She smoothed her fingers along her jeans in a nervous gesture, then sat up to face him, swinging her hair behind her head.

"Ken, we've rushed into this engagement, and we're about to rush into marriage."

"Not the way you're going," he said, kissing her fingers.

"I still feel like we're worlds apart, and now there are other things cropping up."

"Oh? What?" he asked, watching her steadily.

"I have a suspicion that you're so accustomed to overcoming all challenges, that my resistance is what draws you to me."

"That's absolute nonsense!"

"How many women have ever resisted you?" she asked quietly.

"I have never asked a woman to marry me before," he said in a calm voice, but his eyes had darkened in anger. "You sound as if every glamorous woman in the world is swooning at my feet. I'm an ordinary guy in love with a stubborn, misguided, beautiful woman."

"That isn't so. Every time we get on this subject, you tease me out of it, but I feel as uncertain and worried as I did on Christmas Day. What do you expect me to do when we marry? Continue working as a dietitian? Sit at home and wait for you and occasionally travel with you?"

He frowned, letting locks of her hair slide through his fingers. "The latter sounds good to me."

"Well, it doesn't to me. I can't just sit around."

"You can continue to do volunteer work at the mission. You can be a dietitian, but I'd like you to be free to travel."

"And I can't deal with the separations. You're here and there and everywhere except at home."

"I'm catching up on things, and I know right now it seems bad. I'm not always this busy."

She slipped the diamond off her finger. "I don't think you know what you want. I think you want me because I present a challenge to you."

His face paled, and he drew a sharp breath. "How can you do this when what we have between us is so good?"

"It is good and I love you, but I don't think you really know your own heart. I think I'm headed for terrible heartbreak in the future, because, Ken, once I let go of all my worries and reservations, I'll love completely in a way you can't understand."

"Where did all your trust go?" he snapped.

"It isn't trust that's missing. I want a husband who will be home with his family a reasonable amount of the time. You're on the go constantly."

"I told you my schedule right now is worse than usual."

"Ken, you have three homes. I want one home, and a man who will come back to that home at night, not spread his life over half the United States. I've had a lot of time to think about this. You're supposed to be at the airport in a little over an hour," she said softly, trying to hide her hurt because she thought she was doing the right thing. "Ken, we don't have to stop dating, but let's not make it so official. Let's give ourselves—and you—enough time to really get to know each other and see how we fit together."

She placed the diamond in his hand. He glanced at his watch; she saw his scowl and knew he was angry. "I've got to go." He stood up and left the room to get his coat, coming back to face her. "Are you going to let me kiss you good-bye?"

"Of course," she whispered, hating the finality of his words, hating what she had done, wanting to take the ring back. But she couldn't marry him the way things were. She clenched her fists and wrapped her arms around his neck.

"You're crying, dammit, and all because of funny notions in your head!"

"It isn't a funny notion to want you home with me at least half the time. And I want you to take enough time to be sure." She kissed him, silencing his protest. His arms tightened, and he kissed her in return until she was trembling with desire.

He swore and yanked off his coat, tossing it down on the sofa. He was angry, frustrated, and impatient, unaccustomed to coping with arguments such as Camilla had presented. He hurt, and it made him furious. "Dammit, I'll miss my plane! You stand there and cry and say you love me, and in the same breath you're so absolutely sure I don't know my own mind and I don't love you!"

"Catch your plane! Go ahead."

"Camilla," he said biting off the word, "I've told you I have a horrendous schedule coming up. I can't spend time with you like I did at Christmas, and I despise halfway measures. Will you marry me?"

Silence fell between them, and she knew he was giving her an ultimatum. She was torn between what she wanted to do and what she thought was wisest, because she couldn't accept that he was madly, permanently in love with her. Caution and habits carried more weight, and she shook her head.

"I can't say yes now."

"So that means no." His eyes were dark as stormclouds, and a muscle tightened in his jaw as he leaned forward and gave her a quick, light kiss. "Good-bye, Camilla."

Eleven

She watched him stride angrily away, his dark overcoat contrasting with the whitness of the snow, the only sound the snow crunching beneath his feet. The moment was etched permanently in her memory, along with others: the black rental car, circles of light and shadow thrown across the banks of snow, Drifter trotting at his heels.

But no matter how badly she hurt, she felt she had done the right thing. If Ken loved her the way she loved him, he would be back someday. It might take a while, but he would come back. And if he didn't, then it was best to have discovered it now, before they were married and had children. She closed and locked the door and moved through the house, her vision blurred by tears.

The next week the pain didn't lessen; it got worse. She missed him more than she would have thought possible. His photo was in the paper beside an article about him during the last week of January. He was moving his corporate headquarters to Denver, and she knew he was living there now. The following week she ran into him while she was having dinner with Claire. They had stopped at Louie's to eat jambalaya, and as they threaded their way through the crowd toward the door Ken and a beautiful blonde came through the entrance.

Camilla's heart lurched and seemed to stop when she spotted him. The piano music, the noises of dishes and conversation, all faded. There was Ken, looking more handsome than ever, his dark hair combed into smooth waves, his white shirt startling against his tan skin, a charcoal suit and his topcoat adding to his air of elegance. The muffler she had given him for Christmas was around his neck, and Camilla hurt so badly, she could barely catch her breath. She forgot about Claire and just stood still, momentarily startled, unable to stop looking at him.

Taller than most of the people in the crowd, he could see over heads easily; his gaze swept the room and stopped, focusing on her. Ken said something to the blonde woman and she nodded as he left her and came toward Camilla.

"Just a minute, Claire, and I'll be right with you," Camilla said to her friend without taking her eyes from Ken.

"What? Oh, I'll wait outside and warm up the car."

"How are you?" Ken asked.

"I'm fine," she said quietly, clenching her fists

in her coat pockets because she ached to reach out and touch him.

"Quite a crowd."

"Yes," she answered.

"Are you all right?"

"Yes," she answered. *Except I adore you and I want you and I miss you.* "I saw in the paper that you're moving your headquarters here."

"Yeah. And I'm selling my big house. Somehow I lost interest in it."

The news shocked her. There was an awkward silence, and then she said, "It was nice to see you."

"Yeah, Camilla."

Tingling from having his gaze on her, she pushed open the door and climbed into Claire's car, hurting more than ever before.

The hurt increased when she ran into him again at the movie theater and saw he was with the same blonde. This time they were in the lobby waiting for the next show to begin. Camilla was with her friend, Mary White, who worked at the mission. "There's your man," Mary said, and Camilla nodded helplessly.

"I saw him come in," Camilla said. He took his date's arm, and Camilla was staring at him when he spotted her. They would pass each other in seconds.

Mary waved at him and leaned close to Camilla. "I want to get popcorn before the show." As she wound through the crowd Mary stopped to talk to Ken a moment, and then he was in front of Camilla.

"Hello, Camilla. We meet again. We always did like the same places. I want you to meet Kate Madison. Kate, this is Camilla Blake."

"How do you do?" Camilla said politely, hearing her own voice as if it came from far away. "How are you, Ken?"

"Busy. I work in Colorado now." He was dressed in the red sweater she liked, and locks of unruly hair tumbled over his forehead.

"I know. I read about you in the paper."

"How's Drifter?"

"He's fine."

As the crowd poured out of the theater the doors were opened for the next group, and Ken had to leave her.

"See you," he said, and winked.

She waited for Mary to join her, watching him as he moved toward the open doors. The same hurt she had experienced before when she had crossed paths with him became monumental, because he was with the same woman he had been with at Louie's Cajun Bayou! In less than a month he had found a steady replacement for her and Camilla was crushed to think she had gone out of his life so easily. She was amazed at how devastated she felt to discover he had found someone special so soon, but then she remembered how swiftly they had fallen in love. Only for her it had been lasting.

She couldn't concentrate on the movie, conscious of Ken seated rows ahead of her, his arm casually draped across the back of the blonde's seat. Occasionally he'd lean close and say something to her. Camilla ached with longing.

That night she stood at the cold window and looked out across the snowy yard while memories swirled and eddied in her mind like mist. She remembered him everywhere she turned: Ken in front of the fire, Ken throwing a snowball, Ken holding her close in bed.

In April he would be going to Japan. Would he rush to propose to this woman?

Drifter crossed the room and sat at Camilla's feet.

"She might not be so uncertain," Camilla said, wishing she had felt more sure, missing him terribly. She scratched Drifter's head, and when he headed for the back door, she followed to let him outside. The snowman was still there, slightly crumpled from the sun, but still discernible. All Camilla could see was the image in her mind of Ken working furiously to build it and the splatter of snow on his neck and hair when she'd hit him with a snowball. And the lovemaking afterward.

She closed and locked the door through a blur of tears and tried to read some menus she had planned for work.

Wednesday night she was at Louie's with Claire again when she heard her friend say, "Are you sure he isn't following you?"

"Who? Oh!" She glanced at the door and saw Ken. He was with Kate again.

"No, he's definitely not following me. Kate's with him."

"I see. Are you ready to go?"

"Yes," she said, thinking she was torn between

wanting to escape seeing him with Kate and wanting simply to be near him.

Camilla saw him with Kate twice the following week. She started to wonder if they were gong to frequent the same places from now on while he lived in Denver. She was absolutely miserable. She loved him to a depth she hadn't dreamed possible, and if his ring had been on her finger now, she would try her best to fit into his busy world and pray that he continued to love her.

As she sat with Mary one night in Louie's while he was only tables away with Kate, Camilla vowed she was going to stop eating at the restaurant.

"You look like you're on the verge of fainting," Mary said.

"No, I'm all right."

"Don't you think it's odd that we keep running into him everywhere we go?"

"Maybe. This is his favorite restaurant, and I'm not coming here again."

"Good decision, but we'll miss the food. Maybe I can talk them into a carryout. Oh, boy. Here she comes."

"Who?" Camilla asked, glancing over her shoulder, startled to see Kate approaching. She was in a royal-blue woolen dress that was slit to the knee. Her golden hair was fastened at the back of her head, and she looked exactly like the type of woman Camilla had always imagined Ken with.

Kate paused at their table. "Hi, Camilla, Mary. How are you?"

Both answered "Fine" at the same time. Kate looked directly at Camilla.

"Is everything all right?"

"It's fine. I'm happy as a lark," she mumbled, stunned at Kate's audacity.

Kate frowned a moment, looking uncertain. "It was nice to see you," she said in a subdued voice, and turned to go back to where she'd been sitting. Ken was gone from the table, so he wouldn't know she had come over and spoken to them, but Camilla began to feel a slow burn, as anger swept through her like fire.

"That's terrible!" Mary exclaimed.

"She may have been trying to be nice."

"Oh, sure. And tulips grow in the desert. Are you ready to leave? I think I need to get you out of here."

"Yes, thank you."

At the door she felt compelled to glance over her shoulder. Looking across the crowd, she saw Ken heading back to his table, watching her as he threaded his way across the room.

The third week in February the city was hit with a blizzard. Wind came howling down in an Artic cold front that dipped over Colorado, dumping snow. North winds buffeted the city. The big yellow snowplows worked constantly through the day and into the night. Businesses and schools were closed, and Camilla didn't have to report for work, so she volunteered to help at the Sunshine Mission.

She found it even hurt to go to the mission because memories of Ken lingered there. It was as if his presence had permeated her life and would never go away. His image tormented her, and she tried to keep as busy as possible.

She kept Drifter in the house, giving him a last pat on the head.

"You stay in the warm house while I go out in the cold, lucky dog," she said, and he wagged his tail. "While I try to forget," she added, thinking of Ken.

Her car had front-wheel drive, and she reached the mission without much difficulty, parking at an odd angle in the lot beside a row of snow-covered cars. Wind hit her full force, and she bent forward, ducking her head, watching her footing. The late winter afternoon was already dark, and the wind chill was at twenty below zero. The cold took her breath away, and she pulled her muffler over her nose.

She slammed the back door of the mission, stamping snow from her boots while she pulled off her gloves.

"Hi, little lady," Charlie said, seated on a new bench at the back door, and she smiled.

"Hi, Charlie! Think the roses will bloom soon?"

He chuckled and shook his head. "Not this week, they won't."

Ken had donated furniture to the mission and it had been delivered. They had six new beds, two new sofas, a dozen wooden chairs, a new table, and two new benches thanks to him. And he had given money to buy food. She was glad he cared, but every time she looked at the furniture, she thought of him.

She hung her parka on a hook, smoothed out her red sweater, and headed for the steamy kitchen to help with the evening meal. Delectable smells of stew were wafting through the old building, and the warmth began to thaw her chill. At the door to the kitchen she glanced at everyone who was busy preparing dinner.

Suddenly she stopped as if she'd been turned to ice again by the chilly winter winds. As she stared at the help in the kitchen anger began to pour through every fiber of her being.

Twelve

Ken was stirring a kettle of boiling stew, a long white apron over his jeans and heavy-knit gray sweater, while beside him Kate Madison was peeling carrots. Kate's blond hair was fastened behind her head and the sleeves of her black sweater were pushed up.

Disbelief shook Camilla to her core.

Ken glanced over his shoulder to reach for the salt, saw Camilla, and smiled in greeting. Her temper snapped. She crooked her finger and motioned that she wanted to see him.

He said something to Kate, and she took the ladle from him. He crossed the busy kitchen to Camilla.

"May I see you a moment in private?" she asked politely, trying to gain control of her churning emotions.

"Sure, for a moment."

She turned abruptly, and led the way upstairs to one of the drafty empty rooms where they stored the donated clothing that hadn't yet been sorted. One wall was cracked, the boards showing through, and the windows were too dusty to see out of. Unaware of her surroundings, Camilla closed the door behind her and faced Ken with her hand on her hip.

"What are you doing here?"

"I volunteered to help in the emergency," he said quietly. His gaze swept over her red sweater and jeans. "In case you didn't notice, we're having a blizzard."

"You volunteered to help. You really have nerve! I can't believe you would be this callous, this un-feeling! And yet you are!"

Curiosity glinted in his blue eyes as he tilted his head at an angle. "What are you talking about?"

"For an astute businessman you have your dense moments! You know good and well what I'm talk-ing about. How—how can you do this! It's just . . . just downright mean!"

"What is? I don't know what I've done."

"Oh, you don't! Hah!"

"I didn't know you had a temper," he said, look-ing more curious than ever.

"I didn't until I met you! You turned my life inside out and then went your merry way!"

"The hell I did! You sent me on my way, and it damn well wasn't merry! Now what have I done that is just plain mean?" he asked.

"As if you didn't know. I'm referring to your bringing your new love right here to the mission, where you know I'll be!" she raged, and while she noticed his expression suddenly changed, she was too angry to reason why. "That is so unfeeling, so—so . . . terrible!"

"Kate?"

"Yes, Kate."

He pursed his lips as if lost in thought. "If you sent me packing, why should you care?" he asked.

"You know I love you!"

"I don't know any such thing," he said, and suddenly he sounded earnest. "You wouldn't marry me."

"It was because of your feelings, not mine. I love you with all my heart and soul!" she exclaimed, and felt tears threatening to spill from her eyes. Her rage increased because she would be embarrassed to pieces if she cried right in front of him. "You're the one who didn't really love in that arrangement. And I told you you might not know your own feelings. And you didn't!" She was horrified to lose control, but she couldn't stop the words that were pouring out. Never before in her life had she lost control to such an extent.

"Look at you—you had a new woman at your side in . . . only weeks, days!" She snapped her fingers at him. "Zip! Just like that, you have a new woman in your life! Are you engaged yet?" she asked, shaking because she was trying so hard to keep from crying or shouting at him.

He seemed to be biting back a grin while she was fighting tears, both of which added to her fury.

"No, Kate and I are not engaged." He moved closer. "Do I see tears?"

"No! I've cried all I'm going to cry over you!"

"And not one damn tear was necessary," he said gently, and leaned down to brush her cheek with his lips.

"What are you doing?"

"I think it's called kissing."

"Oh! How can you, Kenneth Holloway!" she howled, feeling miserable, yet too hungry for his touch to move out of his reach.

"Because I love you, Camilla Blake. Love you madly, passionately, positively. I love you and only you."

She stopped crying, almost stopped breathing, and stared at him while his words soaked into her thoughts. "You're not in love with Kate?"

"Do I act like I'm in love with her?" he asked, smiling, holding Camilla close. Then his gaze lowered to her lips, and Camilla's anger cooled like a firecracker dropped in a rain barrel.

"Ken," she whispered, crying silently, raising her lips eagerly as his came down to meet hers.

His tongue thrust into her mouth in a heated kiss that made her forget anger, cold, Kate, broken engagements, and tears. She couldn't resist. She threw her arms around him and clung to him as tightly as possible, feeling his solid bulk, his warmth, catching the scent of his after-shave, reveling in his kiss!

"I love you," she whispered when he raised his head a fraction. "I made a mistake."

"So did I, love, when I gave you an ultimatum. I'm not accustomed to getting turned down, and I didn't handle it well, but then I wasn't acting out of intellect. I do better at business deals than marriage proposals."

"Oh, Ken!" she gasped, feeling dazed.

"Will you marry me?"

"Yes! Oh, yes, yes, yes!" she exclaimed without a second's hesitation or doubt.

"You'll trust that I know my own feelings when I say I love you and I always will?"

"Yes!"

"You'll put up with a little traveling by your husband?"

"Yes!"

He lowered his head for another passionate kiss and then held her away.

"Let's go tell Kate the news."

Horrified, Camilla stared at him, remembering Kate for the first time in minutes. "I'd forgotten Kate," she said, astounded she could have. "Both of us tell her?" she said, also shocked by his sudden lack of tact.

"Sure. Unless you want to tell her first."

"Now, that is cruelty!" she said, seeing a side to him she had never known before.

He looked startled, and then amused as if the light had finally dawned. "Come along and we'll tell her. She'll be delighted."

This time Camilla was shocked. "Delighted to have you announce you plan to marry another woman?"

"Trust me, love. She will be delighted. You just march right into the kitchen and tell her."

Camilla stared at him mystified, trying to figure out what was going on, because there was no way a woman whom he dated regularly would be delighted to discover he was marrying someone else.

"I won't do it. You tell her, and if you'd rather wait until she's not stirring stew, I'll understand."

"Trust me, love." Ken took her hand and hurried downstairs to the kitchen. He dropped her hand at the door and crossed the room to talk to Kate.

Camilla's nervousness increased as they talked. Kate looked like the embodiment of the kind of woman Ken would choose to love and marry. She was beautiful, tall, and dressed with a fashionable flair. Her eyes were wide, blue, and lovely, and Camilla couldn't imagine the woman taking the news in a pleasant manner.

Kate looked at her, looked at Ken, and smiled. Then to Camilla's dismay, Kate came sweeping across the kitchen and hugged her.

"I'm so happy that you're going to marry Ken," she said in a loud voice.

"You are?" Camilla asked, stunned by Kate's reaction and forgetting the other people in the kitchen and dining room who had stopped to stare.

Ken moved close beside them. "I thought you knew, but now I realize that you don't. This is Kate, my sister, Mrs. Ralph Madison."

"Sister!"

"Didn't you know?" Kate asked, her blue eyes widening. "I thought you knew. Ken thought you knew. He said you've been to his house and seen my picture."

Camilla could only stare. "Sister?"

"You didn't see our pictures?" Ken asked. "They're all over the house."

"I saw a picture of you and your brothers and sisters, but all of you looked about five to twelve years old."

Kate rolled her eyes. "He's been going places where he hoped to see you. I really think he wanted to see if you were going out with someone else, and here you thought— Oh, Camilla, you ought to dump the whole kettle of stew over the big lug!"

"Oh, no!" Ken snapped. "I'm marrying this lady. No more arguments and no stew!" Ken stated firmly.

"Your sister!" She thought of the agony she had gone through. "You knew I didn't know she was your sister!" she said.

He laughed. "You do now."

"I think you let me suffer on purpose—"

"I think you're getting angrier by the second."

"I don't blame her," Kate said, looking at Camilla. "No wonder you were so unfriendly when I came over to talk to you in the restaurant."

"You did what?" Ken asked.

"I thought you needed help," Kate said smugly. "Then Camilla was so aloof, I went scurrying back to our table. My husband's in Europe on business and I'm between jobs, so I came to visit my big brother. My dumb big brother," she said, smiling as she moved back toward the stew pot.

"All this time . . ." Camilla said, glaring at him. "When I think what—"

"There's one way to end this and save myself," Ken said, interrupting her to slip his arms around her and kiss her soundly.

Camilla started to protest, but it was stopped by his lips, and then to her embarrassment she heard claps and cheers from people in the dining room and kitchen. She pushed against Ken's chest, and her cheeks burned.

Instead of releasing her, he merely kissed her more passionately until she forgot the whistles and cheers and put her arms around his neck to kiss him back.

When he broke their embrace, she stared at him a moment, dazed from his kisses, blissful over the turn of events. He grinned.

"I get my way at last!"

"Thank goodness! But Kate's suggestion about the soup kettle was tempting!"

They had to shake hands with all the well-wishers in the mission, and then they went to work getting the dinner served.

It was one in the morning when they climbed into Ken's new Jeep. He drove Kate to his apartment and then he drove Camilla home, where he climbed out and went inside with her. He dropped his coat on a chair and pulled Camilla into his arms.

She came to him eagerly, her heart thudding with joy. "Your sister! You knew I didn't know! You're always able to read my thoughts like an open book."

"I was a little hotheaded, giving you an ultimatum like I did. I'm used to getting my way."

"Especially with women," she said dryly.

"Don't interrupt me. And especially not with the important one-and-only woman. I made myself give you the time you seemed to think I needed. Honey, I've known what I wanted from that first week. I knew how I felt around you, and it was unique. If you had been out with a guy, I would have stormed your house."

"I wish I had a brother! Oh, Ken!" She stood on tiptoe to hug him, raising her lips to meet his.

"It's just as well you don't. If I'd met you with another man, I'd probably have made a scene," he murmured happily before he kissed her.

Finally he twisted his head to whisper to her. "Reach into my right trouser pocket."

She did, unable to resist caressing him.

"Camilla . . ."

Laughing softly, she groped in his pocket and felt the ring, pulling it out. "You carry this in your pocket?"

"Just in case, love, just in case. You see, you said you don't expect anything, but I expect the best, and I want to be prepared."

"Why didn't you say, 'This is my sister Kate'?"

"I honestly thought you knew. I sold my house in Kansas City, and I told you about it when we saw each other."

"I remember," she said, tempted to add she remembered every word he said and every detail about him.

"Well, didn't you know why I'd sold it?"

"Because of me? No, I didn't. I just thought you were moving to Denver and didn't want the Kansas City house."

"I sold it solely because of you. You said you didn't want a husband who lived over half the United States, or something like that."

A thrill shook her at the intensity in his voice. She ran her hands across his broad shoulders, caressing his neck and touching his hair. "Why didn't you just call and ask me out?"

"I told you, I was giving you time. How's Japan for a honeymoon?"

"And you'll work day and night?"

"No. We honeymoon before I have to be there for work."

"I think for a time now, I'll let you make the decisions. My last one didn't work out too well."

He smiled at her, lifting her off her feet to hold her at eye level. "Oh, yes, it did. Now maybe you've lost all those nutty doubts. I was sure long, long ago."

He let her slide down until her toes touched the ground. He pushed away her coat, letting it fall to the floor, and Camilla felt as if her heart would burst with joy. He was incredibly handsome, and the knowledge that she could go on looking at him to her heart's content for the rest of her life made her pulse drum with happiness.

He paused a moment, taking the ring and slipping it onto her finger. His eyes were the indigo color they became in moments of high emotion. "Will you marry me?"

"Of course!"

"And I want a bride who comes down the aisle to me, looking forward to tomorrow with me, expecting happiness, planning a future and a family."

"Be patient."

"You know I'm not."

For an instant her hand flew to her cheek. "Ken,

there were so many disappointments when I was young."

"There won't be from now on," he said emphatically.

Feeling as if a dazzling sun had come up in her world, Camilla wrapped her arms around his neck, clinging to him, blissfully happy.

He smiled. "Ahh, I'm getting my way. Welcome to my world, love. It's all yours."

THE EDITOR'S CORNER

One of the best "presents" I've received at Bantam is the help of the very talented and wonderfully enthusiastic Barbara Alpert, who has written the copy for the back cover of almost every LOVESWEPT romance since the first book. (In fact, only three in all this time haven't been written by Barbara, and I wrote those.) As usual, Barbara has done a superb job of showcasing all the books next month, and so I thought I would give you a sneak peek at her copy on the marvelous books you can expect to keep your holiday spirits high.

First, we are delighted to welcome a brand-new writer—and our first Canadian author—Judy Gill, with **HEAD OVER HEELS**, LOVESWEPT #228. "The sultry laughter and tantalizing aromas that wafted across the fence from next door were enough to make a grown man cry, Buck Halloran thought—or else climb eight-foot fences! But the renowned mountain climber was confined to a wheelchair, casts on one arm and one leg . . . how could he meet the woman behind the smoky voice, the temptress who was keeper of the goodies? . . . He had to touch her, searing her lips with kisses that seduced her heart and soul—and Darcy Gallagher surrendered to the potent magic of his embrace. But the handsome wanderer who whispered sexy promises to her across the hedge at midnight had his eyes on a higher mountain, a new adventure, while she yearned to make a home for children and the man she loved. Could they join their lives and somehow share the dreams that gave them joy?"

Sandra Brown has given us a memorable gift of love in **TIDINGS OF GREAT JOY**, LOVESWEPT #229. As Barbara describes it, "Ria Lavender hadn't planned on spending a passionate Christmas night in front of a roaring fire with Taylor Mackensie. But somehow the scents of pine tree, wood smoke, and male flesh produced a kind of spontaneous combustion inside her, and morning found the lovely architect lying on her silver fox coat beside the mayor-elect, a man she hardly knew. Ten weeks later she knew she was pregnant with Taylor's child . . . and insisted they had to marry. A marriage 'in name only,' she promised him. Taylor agreed to a wedding, but shocked Ria with his demand that they live together as husband and wife—in every way. She couldn't deny she wanted him, the lady-killer with the devil's grin, but

(continued)

there was danger in succumbing to the heat he roused—in falling for a man she couldn't keep."

Prepare yourself for a session of hearty laughter and richly warming emotion when you read Joan Elliott Pickart's **ILLUSIONS**, LOVESWEPT #230. Barbara teases you unmercifully with her summary of this one! "There was definitely a naked man asleep in Cassidy Cole's bathtub! With his ruggedly handsome face and 'kissin' lips,' Sagan Jones was a single woman's dream, and how could she resist a smooth-talking vagabond with roving hands who promised he'd stay only until his luggage caught up with him? Sagan had come to Cherokee, Arizona, after promising Cassidy's brother he'd check up on her. He'd flexed his muscles, smiled his heart-stopping smile, and won over everyone in town except her. . . . Sagan had spent years running from loneliness, and though his lips vowed endless pleasures, Cassidy knew he wasn't a man to put down roots. . . . Could she make him see that in a world full of mirages and dreams that died with day, her love was real and everlasting?"

Hagen strikes again in Kay Hooper's delightful **THE FALL OF LUCAS KENDRICK**, LOVESWEPT #231. As Barbara tells you, "Time was supposed to obscure memories, but when Kyle Griffon saw the sunlight glinting off Lucas Kendrick's hair, she knew she'd never stopped waiting for him. Ten years before, he'd awakened her woman's passion, and when he left without a word, her quicksilver laughter had turned to anger, and her rebel's heart to a wild flirtation with danger—anything to forget the pain of losing him. Now he was back, and he needed her help in a desperate plan— but did she dare revive the flame of desire that once had burned her?" Only Josh, Raven, Rafferty, a few other fictional characters, Kay, Barbara, and I know right now. Be sure that you're one of the first next month to get the answer!

You can have the wish you wish as you read this: another great love story from Iris Johansen who gives you **STAR LIGHT, STAR BRIGHT**, LOVESWEPT #232. "When the golden-haired rogue in the black leather jacket dodged a barrage of bullets to rescue her, Quenby Swenson thrilled . . . with fear and with excitement," says Barbara most accurately. "Gunner Nilsen had risked his life to save her, but when he promised to cherish her for a lifetime, she refused to believe him. And yet she knew somehow he'd

(continued)

never lie to her, never hurt her, never leave her—even though she hardly knew him at all. He shattered her serenity, rippled her waters, vowing to play her body like the strings of a harp . . . until he'd learned all the melodies inside her. Quenby felt her heart swell with yearning for the dreams Gunner wove with words and caresses. Did she dare surrender to this mysterious man of danger, the untamed lover who promised her their souls were entwined for all time?"

For one of the most original, whimsical, and moving romances ever, you can't beat **THE BARON,** LOVESWEPT #233 by Sally Goldenbaum. Barbara whets your appetite with this terrific description: "Disguised as a glittering contessa for a glamorous mystery weekend, Hallie Finnegan knew anything was possible—even being swept into the arms of a dashing baron! She'd never been intriguing before, never enchanted a worldly man who stunned her senses with hungry kisses beneath a full moon. Once the 'let's pretend mystery' was solved, though, they shed their costumes, revealing Hallie for the shy librarian with freckles she was—but wealthy, elegant Nick Harrington was still the baron . . . and not in her league. When Nick turned up on her doorstep in pursuit of his fantasy lady, Hallie was sure he'd discover his mistake and run for the hills!"

It's a joy for me to send you the same heartfelt wishes for the season that we've sent you every year since LOVESWEPT began. May your New Year be filled with all the best things in life—the company of good friends and family, peace and prosperity, and of course, love.

Warm wishes for 1988 from all of us at LOVESWEPT.

Sincerely,

Carolyn Nichols

Carolyn Nichols
   Editor
LOVESWEPT
Bantam Books, Inc.
666 Fifth Avenue
New York, NY 10103

HANDSOME, SPACE-SAVER
BOOKRACK

ONLY
$9.95

- hand-rubbed walnut finish
- patented sturdy construction
- assembles in seconds
- assembled size 16" x 8"

Perfect as a desk or table top library— Holds both hardcovers and paperbacks.

Nevco US Pat. 3,464,565